Erosion

Of Friendship, Dreams and the Edge of a Cliff

Previous Books

Candle Magic
A witch's guide to spells and rituals
978-1-78535-043-6 (paperback)
978-1-78535-044-3 (e-book)

Poppets and Magical Dolls
Dolls for spellwork, witchcraft and seasonal celebrations
978-1-78535-721-3 (paperback)
978-1-78535-722-0 (e-book)

Guided Visualisations
Pathways into wisdom and witchcraft
978-1-78904-567-3 (paperback)
978-1-78904-568-0 (e-book)

Scrying
Divination using crystals, mirrors, water and fire
978-1-78904-715-8 (paperback)
978-1-78904-716-5 (e-book)

Erosion

Of Friendship, Dreams and the Edge of a Cliff

Lucya Starza

MOON
BOOKS
Winchester, UK
Washington, USA

JOHN HUNT PUBLISHING

First published by Moon Books, 2024
Moon Books is an imprint of John Hunt Publishing Ltd., No. 3 East Street, Alresford
Hampshire SO24 9EE, UK
office@jhpbooks.net
www.johnhuntpublishing.com
www.moon-books.net

For distributor details and how to order please visit the 'Ordering' section on our website.

Text copyright: Lucya Starza 2023

ISBN: 978 1 80341 492 8
978 1 80341 493 5 (ebook)
Library of Congress Control Number: 9781803414928

A CIP catalogue record for this book is available from the British Library.

Design: Lapiz Digital Services
Cover picture by Su Jolly

UK: Printed and bound by CPI Group (UK) Ltd, Croydon, CR0 4YY
Printed in North America by CPI GPS partners

We operate a distinctive and ethical publishing philosophy in
all areas of our business, from our global network of authors to
production and worldwide distribution.

Contents

About the Author

Lucya Starza is an eclectic witch living in London, England. Her earlier titles in Moon Books' Pagan Portals series include *Candle Magic, Guided Visualisations, Poppets and Magical Dolls* and *Scrying*. Lucya also edited the community book *Every Day Magic – A Pagan Book of Days*. As Lucya Szachnowski, she contributed to Chaosium's *Rivers of London: The Roleplaying Game* and co-wrote Call of Cthulhu roleplaying supplements and scenarios including *The London Guidebook, Day of the Beast, Strange Aeons* and *Before the Fall*. She has her own blog at www.badwitch. co.uk.

Acknowledgements

I would like to thank the following people for their help in writing this book, from proofreading and suggestions to encouragement: John Davies, Liz Hayward, Pete Card, Carol Tierney, Fiona Lloyd and Jon Kaneko-James. Your feedback and encouragement were invaluable.

Prologue

Always

It began when we found the bones. Or did it? Perhaps it really began before then. I'll go back further. Wind time back through that summer to June 1987. I was 21, had just left university with my degree in literature and I was going to write a book; something great and worthy. Not some trashy thing like a horror novel full of daft cliff-hangers intended to be page-turners, where a bunch of people do something really, really foolish and end up broken. But I was young and knew less than I thought I did. That great work was never written, at least not then. Now, with time and perhaps more experience, I'm typing these words. I'm remembering the past prompted by a picture on the wall of a beach scene, and an old song on the radio, and these are memories I want to keep.

It is a horror story, although at first it might not seem in any way horrific. To start with I guess it's a tale of young people spending a glorious golden summer at the coast, but that ended. Many of the things that happened still haunt my dreams, and I've decided to write them down at last, as well as I can remember. So, I'll make a pot of tea, put on a playlist from that year – the year of the Great Storm – and start typing about when I first met Jo...

Chapter 1

Who's That Girl?

I first spotted her leaning against a pillar in the pub, watching the stage through the smog of cigarette smoke, resting a pint of beer in a glass mug on one breast and smiling. Jo was often smiling when I first knew her. From that initial glance I could see she was probably in her late 20s, strong, curvy, her hair short cropped and natural. Average height, but she seemed taller somehow. She looked the stereotypical feminist in the way she dressed – a pair of denim dungarees, pea-green DMs and a bright red T-shirt. It seemed purposeful. I was at the open mic night at the Golden Lion. I'd gone to the pub to people watch and get ideas for my novel – the one I wanted to write – but I ended up making four friends: Jo, Zoe, Asher and Baz. It was only later that I met Charlie. But that's getting ahead of myself.

On stage was Asher. I only knew his name from when the gruff pub-keeper-turned-MC introduced him. Asher was a slender young man with dark hair and puppy eyes that darted around the audience nervously. His bright, baggy clothes swamped him. He was trying to make people laugh with a comedy routine, but seemed kind of shy, unsure of his timing. The mic whined as he raised his voice above the general chatter in the pub, trying harder to get a laugh.

Asher's jokes rolled over me at first – I was more interested in his appearance, trying to find the words in my head to describe him if I was going to put him, or someone like him, in my book. Then I saw this woman with her confident smile and her amber pint resting on her bust as she watched the stage. I wondered why she was listening to Asher so keenly and I started to switch my attention between her and the performance. I wanted to

3

know who the woman was. Then I noticed the person next to her, close, almost in her shadow, sipping a half-pint of something dark. She was watching the stage too, but casting little glances up at her friend. She was slim with long dark hair and perfect black eye-liner around large eyes. I wondered who they were, the pair of them, why they were there. I moved closer, nearer to the pillar. Then Asher said something that was actually funny and I laughed, and the women both laughed as well, but I must have laughed too loudly because they turned their heads to look at me.

"Do you know him?" I wasn't really sure why I asked that, perhaps just because it was awkward them realising I was looking at them, which I had been.

"Yes," they both said.

"Asher's in the flat below us," said the woman with the pint.

"It's his first time on stage, so we came to listen," added the one with the half.

"He's brave," I said. They nodded.

"I'm Jo, by the way," said the woman with the pint.

Her friend said: "I'm Zoe."

"Hi, I'm Alison, although friends sometimes call me Alice, like *Through the Looking Glass*," I introduced myself. I was always making literary references back then. I was pretentious like that, but Jo smiled.

"Looks like you've got an empty glass," she said.

"Yeah... Would either of you like a drink?"

They nodded and we all smiled then, I think it was that moment we realised we were going to get along.

I came back from the bar with full glasses and we listened to Asher tell the rest of his jokes, laughing and clapping even when the routine didn't deserve it but because we wanted him to do well. It was one of those perfect times when things start to come together, before you even think there's anything to fall apart.

Asher finished his act and wandered off the stage looking kind of dazed. A tall bloke with spiky peroxide hair and a Stranglers T-shirt, who'd been standing right by the tiny raised platform, handed him some pale drink and they both came over. Jo congratulated Asher with a hug then introduced us. The tall bloke, he was Baz, Asher's flatmate.

"D'you enjoy the set?" Baz asked me.

I glanced at Asher. He'd played the clown on stage in his bright colours, but now seemed serious. He looked at me with big puppy eyes seeking reassurance and approval.

"It was great!" I lied.

Asher frowned. "You sure? I was so nervous."

Jo was the one who reassured him. "Of course you were nervous. It was your first time, but yes, you made people laugh and that's all that matters. You stood up on stage and followed your dream, and you'll only get better and better at it." She seemed warm but down to earth too. I couldn't help but be caught up with her enthusiasm, and I liked her even more.

"Thanks," said Asher. He looked down, took a sip of his drink, but was then quiet as the rest of us chatted on. I learnt Zoe was an artist, and passionate about it. She sketched and drew and painted, and hoped she'd maybe find some way of selling some of her pictures to the tourists that summer. Baz seemed solid and dependable, although I thought he was trying to dispel that image with his hard-man-of-punk appearance.

We bought more beer. Zoe had blackcurrant in hers, Baz wanted snakebite and Asher drank lager with a lemonade top – I reckoned he liked to stay sober, and although he'd played the fool, he didn't want to be one. To be honest, I'm not a huge fan of beer although I drank plenty of it that summer. Tea's my thing. I could never finish an essay without a cup of tea next to me when I was at university. That's pretty much followed me all my life – being able to take a sip of tea and buy time to think if words fail me. Anyway, I'm digressing. I certainly drank beer as much as tea in the summer of 1987. Perhaps that was one of the reasons I didn't get far with my dreams of being an author, apart from all the crazy, scary, tragic stuff that happened, of course.

That novel, the one I didn't write, was going to be about the lives of people in a rundown seaside town. It was a little place in Kent that had, in the past, been famous for its fisheries until the fish went away, and famous as a genteel place where well-to-do Edwardians stayed on holiday, although they went away before the fish. It was along the coast from Margate, where lower classes in bygone days might go in a charabanc to spend their pennies at the pier amusements, giggle at what the butler saw and what have you. In the early 20th century this little town had been full of nice boarding houses, where nice people went to recuperate from vague London maladies with discrete sea dips and walks along the promenade at a time when it was impolite to ask what went on behind the lace curtains. But no one had done that kind of thing for a long, long while. By the 1980s the boarding houses were mostly converted to cheap flats and bedsits rented out to the unemployed and under-employed, part of the area known as Costa-Del-Dole.

It wasn't that far from where I went to university. I'd often visited the beach there on days off from studying, driving along the bumpy country lanes in Emily, my aged, violet Morris Minor. Emily had been a gift from my parents for my 18th birthday and I'd named her after my favourite Bronte sister. Perhaps I should have called her Edith, after the author of a short story set in Kent about a car that colour, although she was more famous for her children's books. Anyway, the idea of renting a flat by the sea, exploring the area, and writing about its murky past and dingier present, appealed in a romantic kind of way. I thought I'd found the perfect people to study.

"Are you local?" asked Jo.

"Kind of, at the moment," I replied. "Well, I was at Canterbury – the uni. Just finished my degree. I can't stay on at the halls of residence and I can't face going back to my parents, so I'm hoping to stay down here, at least for the summer."

"So...you're looking for somewhere to stay?" asked Zoe, hesitantly. She looked at me then up at Jo, non-verbal communication passing between them.

"Well, yeah... I'm looking around..."

"Where are you living at the moment?" asked Jo.

"In my car." That was true. Emily was parked up by the seafront, a short walk from the public conveniences, all the possessions from my little college room packed in one rucksack and a few cardboard boxes, and my sleeping bag on the back seat. Not the most comfortable, but there was a kind of rebellious adventurousness to it. There was a short silence. Jo looked thoughtful and I didn't like to break the spell. She looked at Zoe again, who nodded, like they just knew what each other was thinking, then she smiled at me.

"We're looking for a flatmate. There's a third room. It's small and freezing in winter, but that's reflected in the share of the rent and if it's only for the summer... You could come and have a look if you like."

"I'd love to," I answered without hesitation.

Between them, they explained that Jo and Zoe had the upstairs flat in a converted house, while Baz and Asher rented the one downstairs. Jo and Zoe were looking for a flatmate partly to help pay the bills, but mainly because when they had to sign on the dole they couldn't let the Job Centre know they were a couple. Couples on the dole got less benefits. It was easier to fool the authorities if there were three in the flat. I was fine with that.

The five of us rolled through the streets after the Golden Lion had closed its doors. It was night but, being June, was still warm. A gentle sea breeze meant you could smell a saline tang even on the roads a little way from the beach. Briefly I thought of the corrosive power of that salt and maybe I shouldn't have left Emily right on the seafront, but I was too drunk to move her. Number 4 Mill Lane was a shabby Victorian terraced house that fronted straight onto the narrow street. It had peeling paint on the window frames and three worn steps up to the weather-beaten front door. We trampled through dust and junk mail inside the narrow, musty-smelling entrance, squeezing past a pair of rusty bicycles to the doors to the flats and said our goodbyes to Baz and Asher. Baz unlocked the door on the left, while Jo unlocked the other and invited me up the steep stairs.

The heart of the flat was living room and kitchen all in one. It hadn't been designed that way, but some landlord at least a decade ago had plumbed a kitchen sink unit under the window and wired an electric cooker next to it. It must have been some housewife's pride and joy in the 1960s before being relegated here. An equally ancient fridge hummed loudly to the side of that. The wallpaper was 1970s yellow with huge flowers, faded and scuffed. There was a sofa in some floral print stained almost beyond recognition and a green, sunken armchair in a completely different style. A coffee table was cluttered with chipped mugs and plates, an ash tray and other indeterminate things. I spotted a sketchbook, open at an unfinished picture of a bay with bands of sand and shingle and a tall white cliff with trees at the top. I remember thinking it was good, even then. Funny, remembering that now, as I look at the finished version on my wall here after all those years. It's foxed and faded, but still that same view, which I know will always haunt me.

Zoe put the kettle on, gathered mugs and started to wash them under the tap and I looked around. The two other rooms on this floor of the flat were a bathroom and the main bedroom. Jo said the small bedroom, the one to let, was in the attic up even steeper steps. Actually, there were two rooms in the attic, right up in the roof of the house. One was at the back, but Jo didn't open that door. She showed me into the room at the front. Dust and cobwebs indicated it hadn't been used for a while. It was tiny. The ceiling sloped down to just a little way off the floor, with a single arched window protruding out in a triangular-topped alcove. The bed was narrow even for a single, and saggy looking, but I'd been used to beds in the halls of residence so that wasn't a problem. A wardrobe had been squeezed in next to the door in pretty much the only part of the room that would allow its height. A chest of drawers stood on one side, but under the gabled dormer window was a little table and I knew this was where I was going to put my portable typewriter and create my great work.

I went to the table, pulled back the wooden chair so I could stand closer, and peered out of the window. Across the rooftops I could see the moon rising and if I stood on tiptoe there was the sea, just a glimpse, with a line of reflected silver pointing across it towards me in the darkness.

Virginia Woolf, who frankly never knew what it was like to be skint, had said that what a writer needs is a room of her own. She was right though, and this was perfect. This was where I was going to write my great novel, looking out of that window when I needed inspiration, and watching people come and go, tourists and townies and tenants of all the buildings in this long lane. I could see my summer smoothly stretching before me: days of exploration, getting to know people, finding hidden secrets, past and present, then sitting here in this perfect place, typing and spinning my words. It was faultless.

"Do you want the room, Alice?" Jo was standing behind me, still in the doorway.

"Yes. Yes," I said, turning to her, nodding, with a happy smile. Jo smiled back.

This wonderful woman who I hardly yet knew had offered me the chance to follow my dreams and saved me from the horror of returning to live with my parents. That was, at the time, the worst nightmare I could think of. Over the summer, that would change.

Chapter 2

Little Lies

"Yes, mum, I've got a job interview lined up." It was a lie, of course. I was in the callbox by the harbour, on the phone to my parents. I needed to borrow money from them. I was out of cash and nearly out of overdraft and didn't want to default on the rent so soon after finding my perfect room.

I'd told my parents I was intending to stay on the Kent coast for the summer and that I'd found somewhere to live. Mum had exploded. She wanted me home and looking for a proper job, just like I feared. So, I'd lied and said I was looking for work, real work, just down here, not up there living with them.

"Mum, I need to buy clothes for the interview – a good suit and shoes too. It would make all the difference. And if I get the job I'll need to put petrol in Emily and buy food until pay day. Could I borrow some money? Just a bit? I'll pay you back. Please?"

I'm not sure if she believed me, but she agreed to send a cheque to tide me over.

"Well, I suppose we're all young once. Enjoy the summer." She'd seemed to soften, but then gave me an ultimatum: "You have until the end of September, Alison, okay? If you haven't found a proper job – not some temporary thing – then you're coming home, and that's final."

"Okay," I agreed and we said our goodbyes, but inside I was seething. I was 21. *How dare she talk to me like I was a kid?* I thought, angrily, after I'd put the receiver down. But at least I had a few months and I had to make them count.

It was Baz who helped me out with the job. He saw me sitting on the harbour wall, staring out to sea, wondering where to start looking for work. He sat down next to me, asked me what was wrong. He was always good like that, could tell when someone wasn't happy and usually suggested some way of helping. Not in a huggy, emotional, kind of way. Practical. That was Baz. He did maintenance up at the caravan park on the cliff just outside town. Electrics, decorating, shifting stuff – that kind of thing. Apparently the manageress there needed extra help at the bar for the holiday season and he could introduce me to her. I offered to give him a lift up there that day. He normally cycled, but he said yes.

"Thanks, that would be great!"

Beach View Holiday Park wasn't exactly like its name suggested. I doubt you could see the beach unless you were peering over the edge of the cliff, which you weren't likely to do unless you enjoyed taking risks as there was also a big sign: 'Danger! Cliff Erosion'.

Rows of white caravans were parked some way down from that jagged and unstable brink between grassy chalk and thin air. Some of the caravans were more like mobile homes – solid and rectangular, with their own little patches of garden surrounded by miniature picket fences. Most were the easily towable kind, however. Oldish I reckoned, but pretty uniform in style; presumably pitched in place for the summer and rented to holidaymakers on low, low budgets, who didn't want to live in a tent for a week. Right at the far end was a field where people could park up their own campers, but I hadn't seen many in that when we'd driven past along the gravelly lane to the reception office.

The manageress was a Mrs Sweet. Baz introduced me to her, quickly muttering that I was interested in the bar job before heading off to do his own work. I could also see her name on a printed sign behind the counter: 'Mr and Mrs Sweet Welcome You to Beach View Holiday Park. Enjoy Your Stay.'

"Well, Alison, call me Suzie," she said, showing a lot of teeth surrounded by red lipstick when she smiled, and offered a hand with long, equally red fingernails for me to shake. I wondered if her name was real. Suzie Sweet was wearing a bright yellow blouse and tight black trousers. She had big hair, the kind of black that advertisers claim covers 99 per cent of all greys. It was hard to tell how old she was because of that hair, and she wore an awful lot of make-up. But I reckoned there and then she was a shrewd woman who knew her business.

"So, you're interested in the bar job?" She looked me up and down. "Have you done bar work before?"

"Yes, at uni. Student union bar."

It was only a little lie. I did once earn some money serving behind the bar at a function the university put on. It was one of those jobs that students jumped at when they could as they also got to take home leftover buffet food afterwards if they wanted. It had been an event for a local archaeology trust, a day for its members and patrons. There were talks, which I got to overhear while working at the bar. One of them was about Early Bronze Age burials where strange beakers, knives and other grave goods had been found along with the bones. I didn't tell Suzie Sweet about the archaeology event, just fibbed about how much bar work I'd done before. She didn't quiz me about it. She looked thoughtful for a moment, curled a red lip up at the side, then asked if I could start the next afternoon. I said yes, of course.

I had nearly a day to kill before the bar work began. Back at the flat, in my little room, I intended to start writing my book. I sat at my typewriter. I thought about Jo and Zoe and Baz and Asher, who I was going to study and immortalise in my great novel, but suddenly realised that whatever I typed, they might see. I needed to wait, get to know them better, then maybe type two things. One, the public thing, pages I could show them. The other, private, about them. They'd asked me about how my book was going but, of course, I couldn't tell them I was planning on writing about them, could I? So, another little lie.

There's a difference between little lies and big lies. Little lies are the things you say that aren't true but don't matter much. Everyone does it. I mean, not compulsive lying, like the character in those Keith Waterhouse novels, just things that make life go a bit smoother and keep people happy. At least that's the intention.

"Do I look fat in this?"

"No, you look great!" Little lie.

"Is the tea okay?"

"Lovely!" (No, it was horrid: cheap teabags, water from a scaled kettle and too much milk put in too early in a mug, not a cup...but I wanted to fit in so when Zoe'd made me that first weak, milky yet still bitter-tasting drink in a chipped mug, I'd said it was great, and that's how Zoe always made it for me for a long time. You can't go back on it, can you? Unless you really want to hurt someone, when you're angry...)

"What's your book about?"

I'd told them I wanted to write about the coast and that was true. The great book I was going to write was going to be called *Longshore Drift*. I thought that was original, although now there are several with exactly that title. If there was one thing I'd learnt doing my literature degree, it was that all the good works of fiction are full of stuff with more than one meaning. They have plays on words and hints of deeper significance than the obvious. So, the dictionary definition:

Longshore drift: Noun: the movement of material along a coast by waves which approach at an angle to the shore but recede directly away from it.

Longshore drift is a problem along the Kent coast that people have tried to tackle with breakwaters and groynes. Breakwaters are usually heaps of stones and rubble meant to break up strong currents and slow beach erosion. Groynes are things I reckon all kids snigger at when they first hear the word without seeing the spelling, getting images in their heads of saucy seaside postcards, but actually they're rows and rows of thick poles fenced together. They jut out into the sea to trap the stones, sand and shells, to stop them moving on with the natural flow of the water. The Victorians put up lots. They're still mostly there, with a bit of repair-work, despite getting regularly lashed by the waves.

And, of course, the word drifters applies to people – as well as a kind of boat for fishing with nets. A drifter is a person who is continually moving from place to place without any fixed home or job, usually dust-poor, ground down by life and existing from hand to mouth. That was how I imagined life might be like on Costa Del-Dole. I was wrong, of course.

The word drift has another meaning too, and I aimed to make the title a kind of in-joke for pretentious people who think that kind of thing is clever, like I did back then, just out of uni with my 2:1-that-wasn't-quite-a-first-but-I-wanted-to-make-up-for-it. A drift was also the term used by arty bohemian types in Paris back when Paris was really arty and bohemian. It meant wandering around a town, city or other place where people have built stuff, seemingly aimlessly but actually in keeping with something like the psychic flow of the environment, then writing about things seen or experienced. It took off in English literature too. Iain Sinclair wrote some weird books and poetry after wandering around London. Later, in the 1990s, German writer WG Sebold gained cult status with *The Rings of Saturn*, about a hiking tour of Suffolk, which was really about decay. If I'd written my novel, maybe I'd have pre-empted him. But I didn't. Nowadays I think I'd settle for raising a teenage snigger about a little winkle lodged in a groyne, if I wasn't writing this account, of what really happened.

Back then, sitting in my bedroom at the top of the flat, at my table with my typewriter, my page stayed blank for a long while. Even with the help of a cup of tea. I let my mind drift along the beach in my imagination, but still no inspiration. I stood up to peer out at the sea again, over the rooftops. It looked different in daylight. It was late afternoon and there was a haze over the ocean, so you couldn't really see where the water ended and the sky began. Sitting down again, I couldn't find any prose to tap out in black ink on the white paper curling between the rollers, but I did write a poem, a short one. Even then I knew it was pretty cheesy, although I kept it and eventually tucked it in the frame of that picture of the bay, the one Zoe did and I still have on my wall now. It was something, I suppose, to break the blankness of the page. And Zoe said she liked it when I showed it to her that evening:

A child is playing in the blue sky-seas
With cloud-waves falling about her knees
Building castles in the air with her bucket and spade
And waiting for the wind-clouds to wash them away

The work at the caravan park was hard. Harder than I imagined. The bar itself was part of a single-storey wood-framed building that sprawled along the edge of the site. The first bit was the reception area. Then there was a tiny shop selling packets of bread and tins of baked beans, beach balls and faded postcards and other things campers might need in an emergency. Round the other side, facing the caravans, was a block of toilets and showers. There was a little office marked 'Staff only', but really that meant Mr and Mrs Sweet only. I never saw much of Mr Sweet to be honest, because that office was where he seemed to live, but through the window I saw he was a burly man with a shaved head, probably in his 60s.

The bar building was at the far end of the block and took up the most space. It looked like it had been fitted out at least a decade ago, probably longer. Little tables and chairs made of stainless steel and plastic were crammed in on one side, while on the other there were pool tables, with pinball machines, a cigarette dispenser and a juke box up against the wall. The songs on it were mostly old, like the clientele. The first night I worked there most of the people I served were men of a similar ilk to Mr Sweet. But unlike him they seemed keen to get close to me, leaning over the bar with beery breath and calling me "darlin'". It was a busy night and I made mistakes. Memorising orders and adding up totals in my head while being chatted up by men old enough to be my dad was plainly not my strong point. At the end of the evening Mrs Sweet, sorry, Suzie, told me the till was short. That was my fault apparently, although I'd done my best and certainly not pocketed any change.

"I'm docking your pay for the till error, Alison, but I'll let your other mistakes slide. For now. You're a smart girl, and a pretty one, and you'll learn on the job, I hope. Come back tomorrow night, but wear a lower cut top and put it out a bit more with the customers."

I'd have told Suzie what sweet place she could shove her job if I hadn't needed it, needed the money, needed this summer. So I agreed and swallowed my pride.

I drove back to the flat angry and tearful, but Jo and Zoe were still up and about in the living room. I told them what happened. They gave me a hug and said they'd do what they could to cheer me up the next day.

"Tomorrow, Jo and I could take you to our special bay that hardly anyone else ever visits. We'll have a picnic lunch and go rockpooling, then get back before the tide turns. It's a really magical kind of place, isn't it, Jo?" suggested Zoe.

Jo smiled and nodded. I found myself smiling again too.

Chapter 3

Circle in the Sand

The next morning we set off when Jo said it was the right time. You could only get to the bay at low tide. Nevertheless, when we reached the promenade, the breakers I could see dissolving into foam and spray over the rocks far away at the headland made the route look dangerous.

The way to Jo and Zoe's special bay meant you first walked as far as you could along the promenade. The concrete path on top of the sea wall defended the town from the onslaught of the waves. It formed a hard edge between the town and the encroaching sea, but then wound on beyond the houses. A chalk cliff slowly rose to one side of the path while the drop to the beach below slowly increased on the other. At the end of the promenade there were steps down; not quite the 39 steps John Buchan counted at the genteel Kentish holiday resort of Broadstairs, along the coast, before writing his adventure of that name, but enough to make it a climb. The stairs were probably more like the ones in Lyme Regis, where Louisa Musgrove fell in Jane Austen's *Persuasion*. They were worn smooth, narrow and still wet at the bottom.

Then you walked further along the beach itself. This was harder going. The beach at that point was a mix of shingle and small pebbles, and the shifting surface gave way under your feet so it seemed like you were taking half a step back for every one forward. But to get to the bay you had to persevere, one foot in front of the other around the curve of the cliff that now loomed ominously high above your head and curved forward to a jutting headland between this beach and the next. There were rocks at the base of the cliff too. Some were dark boulders, others were chunks of chalk that could only have tumbled there.

Some seemed fresh and new while others were old. As you got nearer to the headland, in the part most often underwater, the rocks were green and slippery too.

Jo and Zoe's special bay was the other side of that headland and, as Jo had said, you could only get to it at low tide. Well, it varied a bit, usually about 40 minutes either side of low tide apparently, but that depended on the weather and a few other things. In a storm you wouldn't want to try it at all. The receding tide revealed vast beds of rocks of all shapes and sizes around the headland. Some were huge and jagged, some were almost flat, some had dips and hollows that held pools of seawater and you saw micro marine worlds in them if you looked. But you couldn't stop and look for long if you wanted much time on the other side.

So Jo and Zoe and I clambered over the rocks, helping each other and pointing out useful routes and promising footholds. At times we needed our hands to steady us, so it was good that we were lightly encumbered. Jo wore a rucksack containing our picnic: rolls and cheese, a punnet of strawberries and a bottle of cider hastily bought from the little Co-Op on the way, plus a blanket and some mismatched cutlery and plastic plates from the flat. Zoe and I were carrying nothing but our canvas shoes we'd hastily taken off to paddle the last bit. It was windy too, the further out we got, buffeting us and tugging at our hair and clothes as though trying to hold us back. But at last we were around the jagged corner and the sight made it all worthwhile.

There was the bay with bands of sand and shingle and pebbles: a semi-circle edged by a tall white cliff with trees at the top just like in Zoe's picture. We paddled through the last of the shallow waves breaking gently over a stretch of rockpools and reached the beach. We let our toes sink into it, enjoying the sensation of standing on warm sand.

You couldn't feel the wind here in the bay. Not a breeze. It was a sheltered haven from the world outside. No one else was here but us and a few seagulls. All you could hear was the sound of the waves and the occasional caws of the birds. The sky was blue and the sun was hot and it was perfect.

"We have an hour." Jo smiled as she said it, but added practically: "Then we'll need to head back."

"What if we leave it too late?" I asked.

"We swim, although that's a bit risky because of the wind and the rocks, or we sit it out until the next low tide in 12 hours. The bay's never fully submerged except in really bad storms. We've done it in the past. It means you have the beach all to yourself with no risk of being found or interrupted."

That sounded lovely, except that I needed to get back because of my job. I realised I hadn't actually brought a watch, but I trusted Jo. "An hour it is then."

We found a spot to spread our blanket, got out our supermarket spread and our mismatched plates and sat down to eat and watch the waves.

"I'm going for a swim," said Zoe, after we'd finished the last of the sweet, ripe strawberries.

"I will too." Jo stood up. "Are you coming with us, Alice?"

"I didn't bring a swimming costume."

"Neither did we," said Zoe. "We don't bother. There's no one else to see us. That's what's so lovely about it here. No one to care about what we get up to except us. But you don't have to if you don't want to. You can do what you like here."

I decided quickly. "I'll swim too."

We wriggled out of our jeans and T-shirts and underwear and left them in a pile next to our shoes by the blanket, then ran down to the water's edge. There were pebbles nearer the shoreline that you had to watch out for. They were sharp if you stood on them, and once we'd started paddling into surf they were difficult to see to avoid stubbed toes or hard jabs in soft soles. But we stumbled our way further in, holding hands to stop ourselves slipping and sliding; giggling and laughing and

20

shrieking. The water seemed lovely at first, then suddenly icy cold as it reached our thighs and splashed our buttocks and bellies and backs. The level rose higher and higher up our bodies, waves buffeting us and trying to knock us over, but once you'd taken that brave plunge right in you got used to it and it was lovely once more. And we finally let go of each other's hands completely so we could swim in the salty, briny swell, waves lifting us and plunging us as they rolled in, one after the other, splashing our hair and faces with spray.

After a while Jo pointed out that the tide had turned and was coming in, so we let the rolling waves carry us back towards the beach, only putting our feet down at the last possible moment then standing up and feeling the full force of gravity weigh down on our wet bodies, as though trying to drag us back to the soft weightlessness of the water. But we knew we needed to be on dry land with the pebbles and shingle and sand underfoot, to dry off before we headed home to the real world.

"I haven't got a towel." I realised that as we walked back up the beach.

"No, we didn't bring one either," said Jo. "We'll have to let the sun dry us. Just don't lie down or you'll get covered in sand."

Zoe laughed and started dancing. "We can dance to dry quicker. We could hold hands again and dance in a circle – like three witches."

A seagull cawed loudly and a picture came to my mind of the three witches of Macbeth and their deed without a name. I wasn't sure if she was serious.

"Whose doom shall we three foretell?" I looked at her questioningly.

"No one's, but we can make wishes and three's a magic number, especially when dancing in a circle between the tides, that's what Charlie said." Zoe's dark eyes seeming brighter than usual.

"Who's Charlie?" I asked.

"She's this kind of weird druid person. She lives in a little cottage, like you'd imagine a witch's cottage to be, up on the edge of the cliff a way beyond the caravan park, at the end of the road. It really is the end of the road, coz the road just fell into the sea one day, off the edge of the cliff. It used to be further but it's right by the edge now. Charlie's grandma lived in the cottage before her. The council wanted to move the old lady, but she refused to go. Wouldn't leave her home. Then when she died she left it to Charlie. Well, she couldn't sell it. Who buys a cottage that's going to fall into the sea one day? But Charlie decided she wanted to live there anyway. And she does. I guess it's better than her old bedsit, but I'd be scared, personally, living somewhere that could go over the edge in the next storm. She doesn't seem scared though. Anyway, she knows some stuff about magic."

Charlie intrigued me. She'd be someone to write about – another character for my novel. I decided I'd like to meet her.

"I suppose we could make a wish," said Jo.

"So what do we do, if we want to make a wish?" I asked. Zoe looked happy.

"Well, Charlie said that to do magic all you need to do is make a circle and focus on what you really, really want. You imagine what you want like a solid object – so real you can feel it. You can use a solid object and focus on that. A candle, or a wishbone or something. Then you let it go. You burn the candle or break the bone. You have to let it go, Charlie said, so it can come back true. That's why you find so many broken things like swords left in lakes by people back in history. They were making wishes, making offerings to the spirits of the waters so their wish could come back true. But it's even more powerful if you do it in threes, that's what she said."

So we made magic on the beach and thought of our wishes, our dreams, with the salt drying on our naked bodies under the sun with just the gulls as witnesses. We found a stick, washed up driftwood, and drew a circle around us in the sand, held hands and danced within it until we were warm and tingling and out of breath. We chose pebbles that were rounded and smooth and held them in our hands, pictured the thing we wanted to wish for, imagining it as real as we could make it.

"What do we do now?" asked Jo, staring at her stone in the palm of her hand: a piece of white chalk almost like an egg. I looked at mine. It was dark grey, a hard, flattish, smooth oval. I didn't know what it was, I'd not studied geology, although you don't need to know the name of something to appreciate it. Charles, the narrator in Iris Murdoch's *The Sea, The Sea*, collected pebbles just for their beauty. Mind you, he behaved like a sociopath so was perhaps not the best example to think of.

"Let's throw our stones into the sea," Zoe suggested. "We have to let them go, to lose them or break them, so our dreams can become real."

Leaving our circle, we ran down to the edge of the incoming tide and got ready to throw our little pebbles, one after the other.

"I wish the world was a fairer place!" Jo hurled her ovoid piece of chalk into the incoming tide. It sploshed and disappeared into a swell.

"I don't think you're supposed to say it out loud," said Zoe. "I think that spoils the magic. I think you have to keep it secret when you make a wish."

The wave broke and I tried to spot the stone in the backwash, but it was gone. Zoe threw hers and looked thoughtful but said nothing and it was also lost to the sea.

"Is this how it works?" I turned to Zoe, slightly disappointed. Why wasn't there a flash of light or a sparkle of glitter or something. How was this magic and not just chucking stones? But, of course, magic in the real world wouldn't be glitter and sparkles and flashes of light, would it? It would be something so like things normally happen in the normal world that you wouldn't suspect it was magic, I guessed, unless you'd actually cast a spell to make it happen in the first place. And as it was a secret, no one but you would ever really know the truth.

"I think so," Zoe said. "Or you could try skimming it, to make it bounce on the water. I don't know really. I'm not the expert, that's Charlie."

I thought for a moment, deciding on my secret final thoughts before letting go and skimming my stone, aiming for that moment between a crest and a trough. It bounced across the water, once, twice...on the third time it went in and was lost.

Zoe smiled at me. "Three's a lucky number!"

But it wasn't quite three, was it? And the stone wasn't broken. And a stone wasn't a precious thing, like an ancient sword. Real magic isn't likely to be glitter and sparkles and dancing in the sun. I thought with a sudden insight: it's sacrifice. That's why the ancient swords and bones and stuff were broken. And I wondered what I'd have to do, what I'd have to let go of, to make my wish really come back true.

Chapter 4

Faith

"We need to head back. Now!" said Jo suddenly, realising how far the tide had turned. We quickly pulled on our clothes and shoved our picnic detritus into the rucksack. I didn't want it to end. I didn't want to leave the bay, this magical place, and return to the real world. Except it didn't quite seem as though that was the real world – the phoniness of work and little lies. This felt more real, here. The rest was pretending. You have to pretend, and work, and lie, to pay the bills and buy the picnic, so we had to go back to the fake world, but still I'd know the real world existed – in little magical places like this. And that was enough.

We'd left it a little too late. We struggled getting over the rocks and round the headland. The tide was rising and we had to hold on to each other and cling to rocks as handholds so the waves didn't knock us over and drag us back into the sea. We were soaked through by the time we got to the regular beach, and exhausted with the effort by the time we reached home, but at least we made it.

Later, at the flat in my little room at the top of the house, I changed into other clothes. Tight black trousers, like Suzie wore, and a top that revealed a bit more cleavage than I felt comfortable with, but that was the breaks. I moved my typewriter off the little table and put it on the carpet in a corner of the room. I got out my makeup and mirror, setting them where my typewriter had been. I brushed as much of the salt as I could from my hair, painted on my brazen face, and went to work.

The typewriter stayed there gathering dust as the days and nights went on. My little table became home to my mirror, my looking glass, the place where I became that other Alice, the waitress, not the writer.

I saw Baz quite often when I was working. He did all kinds of different things at the caravan park, including helping out at the bar on busy nights – and they were getting busier as the holiday season ramped up. We usually took our breaks at different times because someone always had to be serving at the bar when it was open, but sometimes we found ourselves sitting out the back together. There was this bit behind the main building that was fenced off from visitors, where the empty bottles, barrels and camping gas cylinders were stacked as well as broken things like wobbly chairs and tables and rusty caravan parts. That was where Baz and I went for our moments off. You wouldn't often find Mr or Mrs Sweet there unless they were taking the empties out. Mr Sweet spent as much time as he could in the office that warned 'staff only' on the door but didn't mean Baz and me unless we were called in for anything official. And it seemed Mrs Sweet often disappeared for her breaks into the caravan that she called home, with its picket fence, tiny flower garden outside and bright curtains at the windows, rather than sit with Mr Sweet in the office.

So Baz and I would have a few moments now and then to chat without a huge risk of being overheard, me hugging my cup of tea, Baz with a cigarette. Once, perhaps a few weeks after I'd started at the caravan site, he asked me how the book was going. I told him I was thinking lots, but not typing much.

"My ideas keep changing. Right now, I'm thinking of spending a day down by the beach, watching the rockpools get revealed. I'll find one to watch from the moment the water recedes to when it comes back. Observe what's in it – all the little fish and things in shells, all trapped there together and unable to get out for hours, which might seem like days or weeks or months to things that don't live that long. I'd watch what they do: spawning, fighting for food, trying to eat each other, or just hiding in the weeds to survive between a tide and a tide."

"I like that," said Baz, thoughtfully. "But do you think that's what people want to read – that allegorical stuff? I mean it is, isn't it? That's us, here, isn't it? Don't people prefer to read about other humans screwing and fighting each other rather than fish? Sex and death and murder and that kind of thing?"

"Yeah, I guess," I agreed. "I'm not sure I want to write about that, about death, but I'm less sure of anything these days except that I've found friends. You and Asher and Jo and Zoe."

From our chats I'd earlier learnt more about what Baz did at the caravan park. And it really seemed there wasn't much he didn't do, like he had a finger in everything, including Mrs Sweet.

"Don't say that out loud, and don't tell anyone," whispered Baz when I'd mentioned it. "Mr Sweet'd fucking kill me if he found out. But yeah, I like to make people happy. That's how you get by, pleasing people, giving people what they want. Here I mend things, I fix things, I help people get things... not anything dodgy...maybe a little weed or a little whizz to help people's holidays be a little happier, that kind of thing. I know it's a shit-hole up here, but I try to make it seem a bit less shitty."

"Yes, it isn't the nicest, but it's money, it's a job. I appreciate you helping me get the job, Baz." I'd meant those words, but on the day we chatted about my book, he could see I was feeling at low ebb.

"Alice, I know you won't stay here long," he said. "You're going to write your book and move on. And I'll help you, if I can, like I want to help Asher make it with his comedy routines. I might not know how to write, but just tell me what you need so you can do it. You and the others, you're my friends too, my real friends, and I'll help my friends all I can. You don't want to be around this place in the winter. It's dead."

He took one last drag on his cigarette, threw the butt down and ground it with his heel in the dirt then went back to work. He was right. I had to get on with writing my book and knew I only had until the end of summer.

Chapter 5

China in Your Hand

It was Asher who gave me the idea of asking Charlie to help me decide what to write about, to help me want to get my typewriter up from the dusty corner where I'd abandoned it. Asher sometimes came upstairs for a chat, but not normally in the mornings – he wasn't an early riser. But the day after I'd had that discussion with Baz, Asher knocked on the door late morning. I was the only one up in our flat too, and I was making tea before getting ready for work.

"Hi Alice, can I ask a favour?" He looked nervous asking, but that was nothing unusual.

"Sure, what?"

"Can you give me a lift up to Charlie's? It's just a little way along from where you work."

"Sure. Why do want to see her, if you don't mind me asking?" I'd been wanting to meet Charlie and this was a good chance, but I'm nosey too. I guess all writers are.

Asher looked around shiftily before answering, or maybe it was just his regular nervousness. "I'm stuck. I want to improve my comedy set and I know a chat with Charlie'd help. It always does. She just listens...sometimes while she's doing other things like carving driftwood...she makes stuff out of wood... but sometimes over a cuppa. She listens without saying much. Then, when you've finished, she asks some question and you have to think about the answer, but when you've thought of it you realise you know what to do."

"Oh, I see," I said. "I think I could do with a chat with her too then. I'm stuck with the book I'm writing. And I'm always happy to try someone else's tea. But I'd also be interested in how you create comedy. I'm pretty much in awe of anyone who can write jokes. I wouldn't know where to start. I'm not sure I could write anything funny."

"Neither can I," replied Asher.

I laughed. "But that was funny!"

He smiled, shyly, but a smile.

"Yeah, well, it's a trick really. The trick is to say something unexpected. For a comedy routine you're supposed to lead people along into expecting you to say a certain thing, but then drop in something else, really left-field, at the end. It can be just a two-liner, or long, like a shaggy dog story, but, well not that long. I'm not that good at it. Not yet, at least."

"Me neither, with my writing. I've not written much of my book yet. I think about all the great writers, the ones I've read and studied, and I know I'm not that good. I guess I was waiting for a day when I felt I could just do it, but I don't know if that'll ever happen," I admitted.

"Fear of failing then, I get that. I really do. I always felt like that. My dad wanted me to succeed so much...at school and whatever. He wanted me to be something, someone, I wasn't. When mum was around it wasn't so bad, but...anyway, I don't want to think about that. I got bullied a bit at school too. Being funny, or trying to be, it's a defence. You can turn around your failings, make a joke out of them. I learnt that. It worked with the bullies, but not with dad. That's why I don't have anything to do with him anymore."

"My mum's the pushy one with me. I know what it's like. But a visit to Charlie's sounds like it might help both of us." I put down my cup and grabbed my bag and car keys. "Let's get going."

Zoe'd said Charlie was some kind of weird druid. I don't know whether she was a druid, but she was pretty weird. She lived in a tiny cottage that really did look like some old witch ought to own it, so close to the edge of the cliff that the side window looked right over it, towards the sea. Tall trees loomed at the back, so close you could hear the branches tapping on the roof and walls as though they were testing them, seeking a way inside. In front of it was a garden full of vegetables and herbs and flowers that I learnt could also be cooked and eaten, or sometimes smoked, as well as being infused into tea.

Charlie was in her garden. She was tall with angular features, sharp blue eyes and long ginger hair tied back in a single messy plait. Looking back, I see her the way I first saw her, wearing a navy sailor's cap pulled down over the top of that hair, waterproof and functional looking but old and battered. I see her in her tie-dyed shirt, with plainly no bra underneath it, baggy combat trousers and battered army surplus boots. She was in her garden, cutting the heads off roses and letting them fall into a basket.

"Hi, Charlie!" called Asher as he opened her gate and entered the garden.

She looked up. "Hi! Who's your friend?"

"This is Alice...Alison, only we call her Alice," he said, introducing me. I smiled and said "Hi" too.

Asher went on: "Alice's living with Jo and Zoe upstairs at Mill Lane now. She's a writer. We thought we'd come to see you, if that's okay."

"Sure, I was about to make a brew, come inside." Charlie walked over to the cottage door and opened it.

Inside was stranger than out. In *David Copperfield*, Charles Dickens described a 'superannuated boat' turned into a house that looked on the outside like something more at home in the ocean, but the interior was genteel tidiness. Our Charlie's cottage, on the other hand, had suffered a sea change on the inside. It was full of flotsam and jetsam – bits of nets and fishing floats, twisted bits of metal with flaking paint and strange words just legible through the rust. There was driftwood too, lots of it. Charlie'd shaped driftwood into tables and chairs and shelves and all manner of peculiarities too. Odd things washed up by the sea hung from bits of old rope and netting like strange windchimes. You had to avoid these hanging things as you walked around or you'd constantly bash your face into them, and some parts of the ceiling were so low you had to mind your head on the beams even where there weren't other things dangling.

"Have a seat," she said, and we sat on wonky-looking driftwood chairs at a wonky-looking driftwood table. But although they looked unsteady, they were actually as solid as anything.

"Your furniture's amazing!" I said, looking around.

"Thanks. It's a way I make a bit of money. I craft these things made out of wood I find out and about."

She explained she had this old motorbike that she'd travel about with to scour the coast as a roving beachcomber. Apparently there was a shop somewhere more up-class touristy than our town, where arty day-trippers bought the kind of things she made with what she found. I admit I'd have bought a few items from her too if I had cash to spare and a place to furnish. Maybe not the hanging stuff, but the tables and chairs with their twisty legs and smooth yet warped surfaces, no two the same. They were fascinating. But she didn't make much money out of it. She burnt bits of driftwood in her stove, which was the way she cooked and boiled the kettle as well as heated the cottage. She foraged for food as well as growing it in her garden – nettles and wild garlic for soup, dandelion and lime leaves for salads, and all sorts of flowers she made into teas. It was the teas that really bonded me with Charlie. They were amazing: elderflower, rose petal, chamomile, wild mint, lemon balm and many others. We drank out of her grandmother's old bone china cups.

Tea always tastes better out of a bone china cup in my opinion. The gruesome thing is, bone china really does contain bones. Well, the ashes of bones. Funny, isn't it, that something as grisly as cremated bones would make the finest type of china produced in England? Back in the 18th century, when tea was so fashionable it replaced beer as the English national drink, people also wanted the most fashionable cups to sip it out of. The best porcelain came from China, as well as most of the tea. Both were really expensive to import, but English potteries discovered that adding bone ash to clay not only made the fired tableware stronger, but also whiter and more translucent than ordinary crockery. You could pour hot tea into cups made from bone china without risk of them cracking. Before that, with the incredibly thin Chinese porcelain cups, people had to put milk in first, but refined opinion was that spoiled the drink's taste. I agree. In any case, you don't want to go adding milk to the best blends anyway. And you certainly wouldn't want it in a cup of infused rose petals and lavender, even if to avoid it meant drinking from the cunningly concealed crushed remains of some dead creature's skull.

Charlie's grandma's tea set had a nautical theme. On the outside of each cup was a sailing ship on the ocean – a clipper probably – and inside, near the rim, was a seagull in flight. The saucer had the ship too, but the one on the cup was set against a blue sky while the one in the saucer was sailing into the sunset. To be honest, she didn't have the full set, just five of the original cups and one of them was cracked. Later, when all six of us were at Charlie's place, someone ended up with a chipped blue-and-white striped enamel mug, although they could put it on the sixth saucer if they liked. I never wanted to be that odd one out but, of course, I was sometimes.

But I'm digressing. That first time I met her, when it was just Asher, me and Charlie sitting around her table sipping an infusion of flowers she'd just been picking, I discovered the other way Charlie made a bit of money. Asher asked to buy some of the smokable herbs she grew. I smiled and guessed that was the real bit of comedic inspiration he'd come looking for, rather than just a nice chat. But we did chat. Asher talked about some ideas he had for a new routine, although I must admit I didn't listen too intently to what they were saying. Partly that was because I'd rather not learn all the punch lines of Asher's jokes before I heard them live, but partly it was because my attention kept being drawn to the wonderful things in the room. But then Charlie turned to me.

"So, you're a writer," she stated. It wasn't a question.

"Well, I want to be. At the moment I'm really just a barmaid at Beach View."

"Ah, my neighbours along the cliff," said Charlie. "I must admit I don't have much to do with them."

"I don't blame you," I said. "It's pretty grim there. But it's a job."

Charlie looked at me and paused before replying with the kind of question Asher had said she'd ask: "Grim things that happen to you can be worth writing about, can't they?"

"Yes, I guess so," I said.

I visited Charlie's place often after that. It was a popular place to gather. People would bring cans of beer in the evening and gather around a fire bowl outside the cottage, on the side of the garden by the jagged cliff edge next to the sea. I'd often go along after my shift at the bar ended as Charlie's impromptu parties went on much later than last orders. Someone'd bring a boom box and someone'd skin up a joint. We knew we wouldn't be disturbed. The cottage was past where the road officially stopped, although actually the Tarmac continued right to the edge of the cliff. The end of the road had disappeared one night in a storm many years ago, back when Charlie's gran was still alive. A huge piece of cliff fell away in one go and a couple of other cottages went with it too. You could still see the remains of them down on the beach if you peered over the edge of the cliff: bricks and roof tiles and so on. People had died. The council put up a barrier of concrete blocks across the road some way down from Charlie's gran's cottage, and a sign saying, 'Road Closed'. You couldn't get a car past. I had to park Emily and walk the rest of the way, but Charlie could squeeze through with her motorbike. And that's how things were.

They were good times, those parties late into the night. But I didn't get much more inspiration for my book, even though I thought about keeping the diary of downtrodden barmaid. A few weeks later, I decided to visit Charlie on my own before I started work, to drive up to where the road ended and try to get past my own continuing block, to pick up my typewriter out of the dust and put words on paper. But that chat didn't happen even then. Because that was when we found the bones.

Chapter 6

Down to Earth

Have you ever exhumed a grave in the middle of the night? I guess it might be on the wish list of Gothic poets wanting to follow in the footsteps of Dante Gabriel Rossetti, who dug up his lover's corpse to retrieve verses tearfully buried with her many years before. But it was never something I'd dreamt of doing, and it wasn't a grave in flat earth or a neat tomb in Highgate Cemetery's Victorian splendour that just needed unlocking and a coffin lid prising. The old grave I helped dig into was in the process of falling off a cliff, half exposing a long-buried skull to the light of day. What's more, despite the tales, Dante was too much of a wuss to shift any soil himself. He left that to his friends. I'm proud to say at least I got my hands dirty. We all did.

Only the skull was visible at first. It was a day I wasn't working. I'd intended to visit Charlie later on, but first I thought I'd have another go at writing. I put my typewriter back on the table, made a cup of tea and sat there looking at the paper. Then I went for a walk past the harbour wall and along the road above the promenade. The day was overcast. It'd rained hard in the night and a strong wind was blowing over a choppy sea. I took shelter in one of those quirky little cast-iron Victorian structures with a bench inside and glass panels, designed so holiday makers could watch the sea without inconvenient disarray even in the frequent rain of the English coast. A century later they were more often full of litter, smelling of piss and captioned with graffiti.

TS Eliot once sat in a shelter in Margate – a more pristine one than mine I would hazard a guess. It was where he wrote one of the gloomiest parts of his poem *The Waste Land*, about disconnection. Eliot's lines echoed around in my head. How could I possibly hope to put words together in his shadow? Not even the graffiti was worth repeating. I walked back to Mill Lane, the salty wind stinging my eyes, then got in my little violet car and drove to where the road was blocked, parked and hiked up to the cottage. Charlie was at home, but she wasn't in a mood to listen to my problems. She was agitated. It wasn't like her. She seemed almost scared when she opened the door after I knocked.

"Oh, Alice, it's you... Come in," she said, but she looked worried.

I entered the cottage. Charlie glanced almost furtively behind me, back down towards the road, before closing the door. Gardening tools sat on the table: trowels of various sizes and a kind of forager's basket called a trugg. There was also a long coil of rope – plainly salvaged from the sea but still thick and serviceable – and a piece of fishing net. She seemed to have been cleaning the trowels and sharpening them. Charlie turned and looked at me pensively, as though she was considering something, but she didn't say anything for a while.

"Is everything okay?" I asked. She didn't answer immediately, just stared at me more. I was beginning to feel uneasy. "What's the matter?"

"Can I trust you, Alice? Can I trust you to keep a secret if I ask you to promise?"

"Yes, of course," I said. I mean, you always say yes when someone asks that question don't you? You aren't going to say, "I'm lousy at keeping secrets, so don't tell me whatever juicy news you have to share," are you? No, you tell the little lie. But I did keep the secret, mostly, for many years. I'm sharing it now though, by writing this down. No one keeps a secret forever, do they? Especially when events have happened that show it was a really bad idea. But when I said yes Charlie looked relieved.

"Come with me," she said.

She put on her sailor's cap and a waterproof jacket and left the cottage. In curiosity rather than in trepidation, I followed her out and into the woods that ran along the edge of the cliff, over the other side of the road, just before the Tarmac disappeared into nothingness. She led me along a narrow trail between the trees, more a desire-path than a beaten track. The wood seemed dark, gloomy and oppressive. Little sunlight seeped through the foliage of sycamore, alder and hawthorn that grew dense despite exposure to the sea winds. After a while she took us off the trail to one side, ducking branches and pushing through undergrowth. Our progress had to slow to avoid scratches, but I knew we were heading towards the edge of the cliff. Just before we got there, the sun momentarily broke through. Rays of light pierced the green canopy, sparkling on rain-droplet-weighted leaves that gently danced in the wind, which suddenly seemed warmer. The wood was beautiful now, I thought. Or perhaps sublime like Ann Radcliffe might describe it, a beauty sleeping on the edge of horror as we both inched closer to the brink of the not-yet-visible cliff. We were going slowly, carefully, feeling the ground with toes to check the soil was solid before stepping. But that's where we were going. When we were out of the trees, right at the brink, Charlie pointed over the precipice.

"Look. Down there."

As she said it, the sun slunk again behind the clouds and I shivered. I'm not scared of heights – of looking down a sheer drop from high places – but I could see that the place near where Charlie was standing had recently fallen away. Very recently. Tufts of grass and the roots of trees hanged precariously off the edge and you could see bare earth and white chalk. It certainly wasn't safe, but I edged closer.

"You have to look down," she insisted.

So I did, and I saw what she was pointing at. A metre or so down was a skull, bare of flesh and brown of hue, its empty eye sockets looking from the cliff face and out to sea. I moved back to safer ground.

"You should call the police."

"No," said Charlie. "And you won't either. You promised."

I realised I had, but I still argued. "Why not? It's a body. Dead. I mean long dead, like a skeleton. Or at least a skull from a skeleton. You have to call the police. That's what you have to do, so they can investigate. In case it's murder or something." I looked at Charlie, varied concerns and wild imaginings anxiously chasing through my own skull. She looked back at me, thoughtfully. Neither of us said anything for a while, until Charlie eventually broke the pregnant silence.

"I don't have a phone. And you're not going to phone them. We'll go back to the cottage, now you've seen it. We'll have a cup of tea, then you'll get the others. And we'll talk about it. Together. Don't tell them what you've seen or what I've shown you until they get here. Do you understand?" Charlie's face looked hard and set. I'd not seen her look that way before.

"Okay," I agreed at last, and that's what happened.

Jo, Zoe, Baz, Asher and I sat around the twisted driftwood table with Charlie in her cottage. The rain had started again and was rattling on the windows while the wind found ways to gust under the door and through other cracks. We drank tea. I had the tin mug that day, I recall.

"So, what do you all think we should do?" asked Charlie.

"I agree we can't call the police," said Jo. Others nodded. I kept still and quiet. I thought we should, but it wasn't my decision and I'd promised, and I was clearly outnumbered. I wondered what I didn't know.

Jo continued: "But someone else might, so we need to do something."

"How long's the skull been peering out of the cliff?" asked Zoe.

39

Charlie looked thoughtful. "I'm pretty sure it wasn't visible a few days ago, as that was when I last went that way. There was a rock fall last night, a little one, during the rain. The skull must have been just behind the surface."

"But if you've seen it, it'll only be a matter of time before someone else does. A dog walker or a tourist on a hike. Then they'll call the police for sure. We have to do something. We don't want them here," said Baz.

"We have to remove it, don't we? Even if it means dangling down a cliff to get it, I reckon." Jo's suggestion gained her wide eyes from Zoe and Asher.

"I'm not doing that, no way," said Zoe.

"There's no way I'm doing that either," Asher agreed, speaking for the first time since we'd sat at the table.

"We could wait until it falls out onto the rocks below. More rain like this and it could happen," suggested Baz.

Jo shook her head. "More chance someone'd find it too."

Asher was looking increasingly nervous. "Who is it, Charlie, whose is the skull? Is it someone like a hiker, or one of the people who lived here a long while ago and just died, or was someone murdered and buried there?"

So, Asher doesn't know any more than I do, I thought. I don't know what my face showed, but inside I was panicking. I mean, I'd been sworn to secrecy. What secret though? Surely Charlie or Baz or one of us wasn't a murderer. They looked at me, as though expecting me to say something. I took a sip from my mug to buy time as I thought it through. I remembered that talk I'd heard about Bronze Age burials at the archaeology trust event, back at uni. I'd seen slides of burial sites with skulls and bones dug out of Kentish soil. "I think the skull's old, very old. I think it's archaeology."

Surely that was better than my fears? More likely even. I went on: "It's important it isn't lost, even though I know you don't want the police here. At least that's what I think."

They were all staring at me still, until Asher broke the silence. "So, could we get some archaeologist to dig it up then, without calling the police…"

"No." Charlie crossed her arms.

Jo nodded. "I'm sure they'd have to call the police just to check it wasn't a murder or a missing person and even so there'd be people trampling all over the place."

"We can't trust anyone, except each other," said Baz.

"It's more than that," said Charlie, slowly but firmly. "I agree the skull's old, ancient. In reality she should be left where she is, where her people buried her, not dug up and chucked into a box in a museum away from her land and home, away from the sea. People honoured their ancestors and buried their dead in their own way. They intended them to stay there. Ancient people must've known about the way things rot in the ground and the way the earth changes over time – they'd know it more intimately than we do. They buried her here for a reason and she shouldn't be moved. But we also have to be practical. If we leave her where she is, someone'll report seeing her and we'll have police crawling all over the place – which isn't going to happen. Then archaeologists will dig up my wood and my garden and make a mess of everything, and I might be forced to move out. It isn't like the council hasn't been trying that for years. This is all the excuse they'll need, even if they don't find my hidden weed or poke around in what I'm growing."

Everyone was silent again, glancing at each other, not saying anything for a while after Charlie had finished, but I felt a rush of relief. Of course, it all made sense to me then. I'd been naïve. But I shouldn't have been, really. Of course we couldn't give the police an excuse to nose around, I realised.

"Okay," I said. "But if we are going to move the skull, we have to do it carefully and properly. We have to mark the position on a map. Then we have to take a photo of where it is, a photo of it in place. Then someone has to really carefully dig it out and we have to keep it safe – just in case archaeologists need to know in the future."

"Yes," agreed Charlie. "That's why I've been sorting out trowels and the trugg and the rope and things. Because someone's going to have to go over the edge."

I drew the short straw. It wasn't exactly that. We didn't do it like the crew of the doomed whaling ship the Essex, deciding who would live and who would die – the gruesome incident that inspired Herman Melville's *Moby-Dick*. It was more that I became the obvious choice. It had to be someone light, so that meant me or Zoe or possibly Asher, but they were too frightened. Oddly, I felt kind of excited, curious even. The terror came later.

I got my map from the car, and Baz knew where he could find a Polaroid camera with film. We walked out to the cliff edge to mark the spot and take photos, but soon realised we'd have to wait until the rain stopped and the wind died to attempt to dig the skull out, because we weren't going to be reckless. Retreating to the cottage, we plotted and planned. Charlie knew how to tie a rope for a climbing harness. We'd tie the other end to a sturdy tree and everyone else would be there to help let me down – and haul me up. The trugg would be lined with something soft to wrap the skull in, then the net put in and lowered separately with the trowels. But outside the wind and the rain didn't abate until long after sunset, and we waited even longer before we felt ready. It was a dark night, too. Perhaps it was for the best. Even less chance of anyone spotting us latter-day resurrectionists.

With Asher's bicycle headlamp in my pocket to light what I was doing, I was slowly lowered over the edge of the cliff. The first bit was the most nerve-racking part as my legs left solid ground and I could feel the wind around my ankles. Discomfort came after. The harness dug in painfully and I bumped against the rocks with dirt and chalk and dust in my face and in my nostrils. I could hear the waves crashing on the rocks below, invisible in the darkness. That was probably for the best, but in truth looking down or up made me feel giddy, so I just looked forward, at the fraction of the escarpment right in front of me. The skull had appeared to be so near the top of the cliff when I looked over, but being lowered to the spot seemed to take forever. I gripped crevices with my hands to steady myself, but they were crumbly and full of loose soil. I was unsure where to put my feet. Although I wanted to feel solidity under them, I didn't want to damage the very thing I'd come to rescue.

"How much further?" I shouted up.

"Not far, you're nearly there!" called Zoe.

I heard Charlie's voice as well: "Just a little way more now."

Then Jo offering more reassurance: "You're doing great."

I breathed deeply, fear starting to rise in me, there, dangling over the edge of a cliff on just an old rope, even though I knew my friends were all there for me, above me, making sure I would be alright. *I trust them, I trust them, I trust my friends*, I thought to myself and I took another deep breath, tasting the tang of salt and soil as I did so. The rope lowered a little more and there I was, suddenly, face to face with the skull, staring at me out of the chalk, dark eye sockets in line with my own eyes.

"I'm there!" I shouted. I could hear the others cheering, then the sounds of movement from above.

"I'm going to lower the trugg, with the trowel and stuff," said Charlie. "Don't loosen the earth until you get it."

The cliff face in front of me seemed loose already I thought, fragments fell as I touched the surface.

"Don't take too long, please!"

"Lowering it now!" Charlie called out, but it still seemed an age before it reached me. I could hear the basket being lowered on the rope as it brushed against the dirt and chalk above me. Dust and other indistinguishable fragments dislodged, fell on my face and head, reminding me how fragile the cliff was. But at last the trugg was far enough down to where I could see it and use it.

Slowly and carefully, I started to remove the chalky soil from around the jaw and cranium. It was crumbly. I used the trowel, but also my fingers to ease the skull out, bit by bit, carefully. This close, she was so real, someone who had once been alive. I was terrified of breaking her, more terrified than I was of falling. In fact, I became so absorbed in my task that I almost forgot my perilous position and the rope cutting into me, the cold sea air around me and the waves and rocks below. Almost. It was slow work. I was unsure exactly what the time was when we started, but nights are short at the height of summer. I gradually became aware that the light was increasing, just a little, as finally the skull came away from its grave and into my hands. It was a strange feeling, like I was setting someone free, or perhaps even giving birth; bringing new life into the world just as a night was ending and a day was dawning. I swaddled the skull in the green shawl in the trugg and watched her be lifted to safety. And then felt elated as my friends finally hauled me back up and over the edge of the cliff onto firm ground once more. Everyone was smiling.

"You do realise, there'll probably be more bones. A bit deeper in. The rest of the skeleton perhaps," said Jo, as we walked back to the cottage, the skull safely wrapped in her shawl in the basket.

Charlie nodded. "Of course. We'll have to look for them."

During the next few days we revisited the site of our excavation on the cliff to see if more bones had been revealed. We retrieved all we saw.

Chapter 7

Crazy Crazy Nights

The exhumation was a gradual process, over several nights. We got into the habit of starting at first light when no one else would be around then hiding our diggings before the day had started. It isn't that we were early risers. We weren't. We'd turn up at Charlie's over the course of the evening and stay after any other visitors had left. At first we were like a gathering of conspirators, meeting by oil lamp late into the night and plotting, but later it seemed we were more some sort of secret cult.

Charlie'd hidden the skull away in a wooden cupboard on the wall with doors that locked behind a little key. She put the skull right at the back with a row of books in front of it so it just looked like a bookcase. I'm always interested in what books people have; it says a lot about them. Charlie's were mostly practical: *Carpentry for Beginners, Whittling and Woodcarving, Food for Free, The Foraging Pocket Guide,* some cookery and gardening books, a battered old dictionary and the like. She had a dog-eared paperback edition of *Zen and the Art of Motorcycle Maintenance,* the book that launched a thousand metaphysical road trips in the 1970s, and a copy of *The Druids* by Ward Rutherford, I recall. But, when Charlie unlocked the doors and took the books out, the little cupboard became a shrine.

Gradually other bones were added to the sanctum. There were 15 in total, like holy relics. With them we'd found something copper green that might have once been a knife, and shards of a little pottery goblet or beaker, long ago broken. We arranged them reverently, and at night we would open the doors to the holy of holies and raise our beer in her honour. Someone suggested calling her the Bone Mother, but after a while that didn't seem right.

"We have to give her a real name, a proper name," said Zoe.

"Yes, that'd be good," said Charlie. Jo, Baz, Asher and I quickly agreed, but choosing a name took more discussion.

Asher came up with the first suggestion. "Perhaps we should name her after Charlie's grandmother."

Charlie frowned. "No, not my grandma. Her name was Marissa, which means the sea, but I know where she's buried and it isn't on a cliff. Not her name. No ancient skull gets called that."

"I've always liked the name Jennie." I remembered one of my favourite books from my childhood, by Paul Gallico, but as soon as I said it I realised it sounded wrong too. Our skeleton wasn't a stray cat.

Zoe agreed. "Jennie doesn't seem like an old name. She needs an old name. Helen, that's an old name, isn't it?"

"Is it?" asked Baz. "I don't know much about old names, but it doesn't sound that old."

"Well, there's Helen of Troy, the most beautiful woman in the world according to Homer. The ancient Greeks and the Trojans fought over her for 10 years," I said. "It's an old name."

"But we don't know where she came from. I mean what culture," Jo pointed out.

"Why don't we ask her?" We all stared at Zoe as she said that.

"What do you mean?" asked Baz, but I guessed what Zoe was suggesting and I think so did the others.

"Hold a séance and ask her, ask her who she is. Charlie knows how." We all realised that was exactly what we had to do.

I think everyone knows a séance is where people try to contact the dead, but there are different types and ways to go about it. Charlie, of course, knew more than we did.

"I've been to séances, as a child, with my grandma," said Charlie, quietly. "Her husband died on the front, back in the first world war. Spiritualism was a big thing then and my gran was into it. People needed to have a few last words with lost loved ones, or at least try. When my mum – her daughter – died, gran took me along. There are fakes and frauds, of course, but sometimes it works. I know what to do.

"You can have someone tune in psychically and turn messages from beyond the grave into words for the living to hear. They go into a trance and channel ghosts. Some translate, some let the spirits possess their body – let them speak through their lips. Some go further and help the ghosts make ectoplasmic heads and hands, to reach out to those they've left behind."

Baz interrupted. "No fucking way am I being groped by some gloopy dead person." The rest of us giggled, but the looks of horror on our faces showed none of us wanted that either.

"Well," said Charlie, "the simplest way is to use a spirit board."

We'd all heard of them, of course, but there's a lot of misunderstanding about what they really are. Spirit boards were invented back in the late 19th century, Charlie went on to explain. I guess there wasn't much to pass away the time before radio and telly, so parlour games of all sorts were what well-to-do Victorians got up to if they weren't just all work and no play. Believe it or not, using spirit boards to contact the dead came under the category of play. Of a dark winter's evening they would close the curtains, dim the gaslights, move the aspidistra to one side and sit around the table to try to chat with their dearly departed aunties. It was very popular – although I understand there might have been more than entertainment as a motive. Apparently the question most asked was: "Where is the money hidden?"

"Ouija's a name trademarked by a game company," Charlie went on. "Opinion's divided on whether it is just a game or not. A real Ouija board is marked with the alphabet, numbers, 'yes', 'no' and 'goodbye'. It comes with a heart-shaped bit of card called a planchette, with rollers or similar on the bottom. The planchette goes on the board. People put their fingers on it and ask questions, and the planchette spells out answers. It can be spirits, or it can be people cheating, of course."

My only knowledge of planchettes was their unsympathetic treatment in Shirley Jackson's famous ghost tale, but I took in all Charlie said. It sounded better than potentially being possessed. We didn't have a Ouija board, but we knew how to improvise. Baz brought a flat board with a smooth surface from the caravan park, Charlie had a Scrabble game she used to play with her grandmother, Jo brought a wine glass with a short stubby stem from the flat. We put the board on the table and on it stuck a circle of Scrabble tiles from A to Z, 'yes', 'no' and 'goodbye'.

When we were ready, we inverted the wine glass and put that in the middle. The lights from the cottage's stove and oil lamps were always dim. There was no electricity. Charlie reverentially took the skull from her shrine and placed her at one end of the table, facing the board, with a lamp next to her. We sat around the other three sides and put our fingers on the foot of the wine glass. There was a pregnant silence before Charlie spoke.

"Is anybody there?"

At first, nothing happened. Silence except for a few natural sounds from outside: the wind, distant waves and the creak of trees in the wood. Inside the cottage there was darkness all around the circle of light from the lamp, which cast the skull and us, with our fingers outstretched on the spirit board, into a sharp chiaroscuro of dark and light. The empty eye sockets were pools of blackness although I stared into them to see if I could sense some flickering of spirit within.

"Is anybody there?" Charlie repeated. "If there is, guide our hands."

Slowly, the glass seemed to move under our fingers. I know I wasn't pushing it. I'm not sure if anyone else was. It didn't seem that way at the time, it seemed as though the glass just started to slide of its own volition across the smooth board, slowly, slowly, towards 'yes'.

It stopped. We looked at each other, but no one said anything for a moment, until Charlie spoke again.

"Are you the spirit of the skull?"

The glass moved slowly back towards the centre, then stopped, then started gently, gradually, circling. Surely no one could be making it do that? Surely?

"Are you the spirit of the skull? Are you the Bone Mother? Please say yes or no."

The glass started to move straight again, straight to 'yes', then rapidly back to the centre. It stopped. I think we'd all been holding our breath, but felt we could breathe again, deeply, as our heart beats quickened, our eyes still fixed on the glass and our fingers pressing on it.

"Who are you? What is your name?"

The glass started to move again, tentatively, circling at first, then outwards towards a letter – 'R' – then back to the centre. It stopped, then moved again – 'O'. Back again, then tentatively to 'S', then more quickly to another letter – 'M'. Then it sped up more. Quickly, decisively, the glass went to more letters, 'O, R, T, A'. Then back to the centre, stopping.

"Rosmorta," whispered Zoe.

"Is that a name?" asked Jo, quietly.

"Shhh..." whispered someone, I don't remember who, but Charlie addressed the spirit again.

"Rosmorta, we welcome you. We welcome you as our guest. But we know this land we are on is yours too; was yours long before it was ours. We ask that you allow us to be your guests too. We wish to honour you, our ancestor of this place, Rosmorta. Will you accept our invitation, and our company, in all goodwill?"

The glass started to circle, slowly at first, then picking up speed. We were struggling to keep our fingers on it, leaning over the table as the glass circled wider and wider and faster and faster. Then as though the circle could no longer hold it, it spun outward, clunking into the tiles stuck on the board, and off the table into the darkness, where we heard it smash against the wall. I looked down. The letters it had crashed through, loosening them as it went, spelled 'yes'.

We looked at each other, stunned, not knowing what to think, but it was Charlie who gained composure first and spoke.

"Well, I think our invitation was accepted. I think Rosmorta is here to stay."

I wasn't entirely sure that was a good thing.

Chapter 8

Sweet Little Mystery

I didn't tell the others, but the next day before my shift of bar work began I visited the public library in the town. I've always loved libraries, just being among the rows of books fills me with excitement at the wealth and depth of knowledge and countless stories they contain. But also the quietness and solitude give me a sense of peace. When I was at university, I'd loved studying in the library. I'd enjoyed sitting at a desk in an out-of-the-way corner with books all around me and pages open next to me as I plucked their wisdom and penned my essays. Sadly, my ticket for the university library was no longer valid, but I was sure that even the small local library would have some reference books I could use to look up the name Rosmorta.

The library was in a red-brick Victorian building, nestled between the post office and a newsagent. It was only on a single storey, but with the high ceilings of its era. That sweet smell of old paper welcomed me as I walked inside. The lines of metal shelves were modern and mostly filled with popular novels and children's books rather than scholarly monographs or classic canonical works of literature, but it was still inviting and I felt immediately at home. Normally I love to spend ages among rows of tall shelves, wandering up and down the aisles, feeling a sense of timelessness, of moving in quiet reverence down pathways between portals to many worlds. I like to savour the moments while picking and choosing which volumes to take down to open and find treasures within. There weren't that many shelves in this building to be honest, but I still felt a tingle of expectation, safety and excitement while walking between them. The reference section at the back called to me.

There's a form of divination called Bibliomancy. You open a book at random and read a line to tell you what you should do. Sometimes I like to do something like that; close my eyes and pick the first book my fingers touch, then take it to read and learn its inner mysteries. But that wasn't quite what I was doing today. Today I was on the trail of a ghost.

My favourite writer of ghost stories is MR James, someone whose own love of libraries and ancient texts seeped into all his tales of terror, his spectres sometimes materialising from the very dust of archaic tomes. Maybe he'd have had a word of warning to my own curiosity if he had been there to counsel me. But he probably wouldn't. He'd probably have been keen to help, eager as I was to solve a puzzle with the help of books. I didn't have enough time today to wander aimlessly in the stacks of books and it was too late to stall. We'd already whistled up the dead, hadn't we?

The first thing I looked at was a book of names. I guess it was more aimed at mothers-to-be hoping to find the perfect appellation for their anticipated child rather than a book of the names of the dead. It wasn't much use for me. It had nothing quite like Rosmorta. Thinking of older names, I found an encyclopaedia of mythology and discovered that Rosmerta was recorded in Roman times as a goddess of fertility and plenty from ancient Gaul, on the other side of the Channel from Kent. The word was a mixture of old Gallic terms for great provider or carer. But that wasn't quite the spelling we'd got. The end of the name we had seen spelled out was 'morta', and Morta was a Roman goddess of death. I read further and learnt she was one of the Fates, along with her two sisters. Nona spun the thread of people's lives, Decima measured the length and Morta cut the thread and chose the manner of a person's dying.

It seemed kind of right, but I still wasn't sure. Surely a human body buried in a normal grave wouldn't be any kind of goddess. They'd just be like anyone else. And for some reason

I'd thought our skull was older than Roman, but then again, I'm not an archaeologist. I began to wonder if what we'd raised was really the spirit of the skull or something different, something more powerful, even something dangerous. Or perhaps our ancient spirit *was* a protector and would provide for us and grant us our desires. Or maybe she was both: protector and destroyer. Suddenly I thought back to that day in early summer, that perfect day, when three of us had cast a circle and made wishes on the beach. I remembered my own wish and the dark stone I'd cast into the sea as an offering. I shut the book, put it back on the shelf and left the library.

Outside the midday sun was shining as I walked down the high street. People were going about their everyday business, shopping, lingering to chat with friends and standing at the bus stop; mothers with children and babies in prams. It all seemed so normal and yet somehow unreal. Again, I got that feeling I had at the beach, wondering what the real world really was. Was it this, or was it the world of spirits, of magic and special places? Or was all that weirdness just the stuff of imagination, which could nevertheless carry you away to be lost down some rabbit-hole of fantasy? *There you go, Alice,* I thought, *living up to your nickname.*

I reached the crossroads where the road to the seafront bisected the road to home. The pedestrian lights were against me and I had to wait. As I stood there, words came into my head unbidden and I ran them through my mind almost without thinking, *Rosmorta, grant me my wish. Take what you will, but let it be.*

The lights changed and my way was clear, but I walked on home wondering what in hell I had just done.

Chapter 9

Shattered Dreams

I went back to Mill Lane, changed my clothes and went to work. For a day or two life went on almost as if it had gone back to normal. But after that came the week when everything changed. First, a letter arrived from my mother.

Dear Alison,

I hope you are keeping well and enjoying your holiday at the seaside. I was hoping you might send a postcard, but perhaps I am old fashioned about these things.

I've been thinking over what we discussed about your future, Alison. I know you are keen to make a career in writing and I agree that something of that nature makes sense following your degree in English. However, you do need to be sensible. You need to get a foot on the ladder for a proper career with a recognisable path for advancement, not a dead-end job or some romantic dream of living in a garret scribbling.

I've been talking to my friends at the Women's Institute. Marjorie (You do remember Marjorie who redesigned our lounge, don't you?) knows the editor of the local newspaper. She said she'd have a word and, guess what? They have just decided to take on an editorial assistant. The job hasn't even been advertised yet. It isn't exactly a writing job as it will mostly be filing, dealing with the post and typing. It is a junior role so not well paid, but it could lead to something. They say for the right candidate there could be training offered down the line, potentially to become a junior reporter. That would be a proper career and something I'd be proud for my daughter to do. And even though the pay is low, you would be living here with us and we wouldn't expect you to pay rent. Your father and I think this would be ideal for you.

Do think this over, Alison. They are going to put the advert for the vacancy in next week's paper, so if you want to apply let me know and I can post you the details. Please don't make trouble over this Alison, think of your future.

All my love,

Mum

I read the letter several times, at first angry, then puzzled. I wasn't sure what to make of it. The job was possibly perfect, but it meant going back home – my old home – leaving my friends, giving up my dreams. Was my wish being granted in some peculiar way? I'd said I'd give anything. But was it really what I wanted? Or was it nothing to do with all that stuff about wishes and bones and ancient spirits, just my mum trying to organise my life for me like she always did, always does, always will if I didn't manage to break away completely?

I didn't want to phone my mother about this. I couldn't face talking to her. I had to admit I couldn't just let the opportunity slide, but the rest? My mum would want a quick reply and I had to keep her happy, keep my options open, so I made use of my typewriter and a dusty plain page that'd been sitting there for weeks and typed.

Dear Mum,

Thanks for thinking of me. I'm well. The job on the newspaper does sound great and I'd love to find out more about it. Please send me the advert so I can look at it.

I'm doing fine down here and have made lots of friends quite apart from the spiders in my garret who are helping me scribble. The job here's going nicely and I'm also getting plenty of writing done.

Hope you and Dad are well.

Love you lots,

Alison

Little lies again, little lies, but I couldn't tell them I'd written nothing except one poem, could I? The job at the caravan park sucked, but it was money and it paid the rent. Soon it was to come crashing down in the most horrible of ways, but I didn't know it then. I got myself ready for the evening shift at the bar, turning my thoughts to that rather than the problem that was my mother. Later, and for a very brief while, it even seemed that Beach View might lift itself out of being a necessary evil and turn into something good.

Sal was 18, with short blond hair and blue eyes and the most beautiful smile, and she liked books. I got chatting to her because of a book, of course. It was Thursday, just gone 5.30pm, and the sunlight had that golden hue it gets in the late afternoons as summer slowly starts to hint that it won't go on forever. I'd just opened the Beach View bar, but it was pretty empty. A few people were outside at the round tables with parasols that were trying but failing to look Continental. Sal was sitting on her own, reading. Virginia Woolf's *To the Lighthouse*. You didn't see many people reading anything actually literary at Beach View. I couldn't help commenting on it as I came up to her table brandishing my pad of order checks.

"Holiday reading, or study?" I was genuinely curious.

"I guess a bit of both," she replied, her blue eyes looking straight into mine, over her paperback. "I'm starting uni this September. This book sounded the most likely holiday reading from what's on my list."

"I won't tell you the ending then." I smiled back, thinking back, thinking how lovely it would be just to go back, start uni all over again and have another three years to read and write and not have to think about what I was going to do afterwards.

"You've read it?" She looked at me with a quizzical smile.

"Yeah. I finished an Eng Lit degree this summer... I'm not planning on being a barmaid here for the rest of my life."

"It's a bit grim here, isn't it?" she said, then looked mortified. "I'm sorry, I probably shouldn't have said that. It's just that I've been coming to this caravan park with my parents every August since I can remember. I think I used to like it here, when I was tiny, but now I dread it. I only came this year because my parents insisted. You know, last summer holiday as a family before I move away and all that. It really will be the last time too, whatever my parents say."

I knew I'd found a kindred spirit. "Yeah, I know exactly what that's like."

She told me who she was and that she was bored and said how lovely it was to chat to someone who wasn't her parents. Almost without realising what I was saying I told her my name and asked her if she'd like to go somewhere less boring tomorrow, with me.

"Where?" she asked.

I nodded at her book. "To a lighthouse?"

There was one within driving distance and in those days it hadn't been automated. North Foreland, on the Thanet cliffs, had lighthouse keepers operating it and running tours. Sal hesitated and I felt panicky in case she said no, but she agreed with a lovely quizzical smile. "If the weather's good enough."

And so we became friends, just as a shout called me back to work.

"When you've finished taking the orders, come back here, there's customers at the bar!" shouted Suzie. I sighed, in resignation this time.

"What do you want to drink?" I asked Sal.

"Green tea?" she asked. Sadly, behind the bar we only had a battered box of PG Tips with a picture of monkeys on the front.

I don't think I'd ever felt quite so happy. Sal and I drove away from the grubbiness of Beach View, along the Kentish country lanes to the lighthouse. The weather was perfect: blue skies, sun and a light breeze flowing through Emily's open windows. We chatted about our parents, our lives, our favourite books, the things we could see all around us. We drove past fields, fruit orchards, sleepy little villages and cottages with gardens full of colour like something out of *The Darling Buds of May*. Pa Larkin would have loved it. We talked about the past, the present but not the future. I nearly did, but the words stuck on my tongue. *Don't jinx this*, I thought. Then we reached the lighthouse.

It stood on the edge of a cliff, stark white and tall against the blue sky with the sea behind it, green grass in front and a cluster of little white buildings at its base, but not much else manmade for miles except a few fences and field markers. We took a tour with the lighthouse keeper, ascending the spiral stairs to the top of the tower and learning about the history of the beacon which guided ships safely on their course through the English Channel. But the talk about lamps and lenses and electrification washed over us both. It was just lovely to be there together, away from everyone who knew us, climbing high and looking out at the view over the water to one side and the land the other with the sky above. We looked at each other and smiled, ready to leave and explore outside.

Down the stairs and through the door, we both instinctively knew we wanted to be away from the lighthouse and its organised tourism. Sal and I went for a walk along the cliff path, found a sheltered spot to sit and stare out into the blue, listening to gulls and wind and the waves below. We shared tea from an old Thermos I'd found in the flat before setting off and filled with Earl Grey. But it couldn't last forever and eventually we had to head back. My shift was starting in less than an hour and my mood dipped at the thought of it. But there would be other days, I thought.

The next night, Saturday, was when it all ended. Sal was sitting with her parents in the bar, looking glum, but I couldn't really go up and say anything. It was busy that night. Later, I went to the back to take out some empties and look for a new keg. It wasn't my break time and I should only have been out of the bar for a moment, but there was Sal perched on a crate. My surprised look quickly turned to a smile.

"Hi," I said. Sal didn't smile though. She looked kind of down.

"I'm going home tomorrow," she said, simply.

"Oh, that's a shame. I mean, I know you don't like it here, but I'll miss you."

"Give me a hug?" she asked.

So I did, and she kissed me on the cheek, then on the lips, just kind of tentatively, soft and beautiful. I kissed her back and for a moment the world stopped and it really was perfect. But then the world started again with a lurch, and everything turned to shit.

"Fucking disgusting!" It seemed Suzie had followed me outside and she was standing in the doorway, staring. Sal and I moved apart, but said nothing.

"This area's out of bounds to guests," snapped Suzie, cold venom in her voice, looking at Sal. "Get back inside and stay with your parents. Do you understand?"

Sal glanced at me, then at Suzie, then turned and left without speaking another word.

"As for you," Suzie said, getting closer to me, "you can leave. Stay out here and I'll fetch your cash for this evening, then go. If I see you talking to that girl again – or I see you anywhere here after tonight, I'll tell my husband. Do *you* understand?"

I did. I nodded, not trusting myself to reply. I waited for my pay, then left. I got into Emily and drove back to the flat. I only wish I'd got Sal's phone number or address. That was among my biggest regrets of the summer.

There was no one in the house when I got back to Mill Lane. I wondered why, then I remembered it was open mic night again at the Golden Lion and that's where they'd all be. I hoped they were having fun, but I was in no mood to join them. In some ways I was relieved to have the place to myself, the silence and the darkness. Although it would have been nice to weep on Jo's shoulder and maybe tell Baz just what I'd like him to say next time he fucked Mrs Sweet, actually I realised I just wanted to be alone. To cry alone. I went to bed and sobbed into my pillow, tears of humiliation, of sorrow, of anger. After a while, I slept. And I dreamt.

In my dream, I saw my typewriter on my little desk by the window, alone in a pool of moonlight. As I watched, the roller turned and a sheet of white paper threaded through. The grey metal type bars seemed stretched, strangely elongated, tapering like spider-legs. The escarpment was oddly raised and the platen and paper rest stark above it as though they were parts of a much older machine. The spindles turned and the ribbon rippled, taughtened. I could smell the tang of ink, acrid, bitter, like old oil and ash. Then the keys started moving, depressing and rising without fingers touching them. They were bone-white.

Slowly, click, clack, click, clack along the lines, the tring-whirr of the carriage return. I got up and looked at the letters appearing on the paper. At first, I couldn't understand them. It seemed they were in some strange foreign language, perhaps something ancient and archaic, symbols rather than words, but then it seemed that although I couldn't read the typed lines, I could nevertheless hear the words like a chant in my mind and they became clear:

By Earth and Water
Air and Fire
Give to me
What I desire
As one sows
So shall they reap
May Justice fall
On Suzie Sweet...

I awoke with a start and I knew what I had to do.

Chapter 10

It's a Sin

I was awake long before Jo and Zoe the next day, but I wouldn't have expected them to be up any time before noon on a Sunday anyway. The house was still and silent, apart from the creaks that all old buildings make but which you only hear late at night or in the early hours when your mind is going to peculiar places and everything seems amplified beyond the natural. Following the strange dream, I'd slept only fitfully. My tears of the night before were over. My grief had converted to anger, but the certainty I'd felt after waking from my dream was wavering, slipping away. A voice in my head was saying to ignore Mrs Sweet's warning and drive back up to the holiday camp to try to find Sal before she left. I should patch things up with her, say I was sorry how it had worked out, wish her well, say goodbye properly and – maybe – get her phone number. Another voice told me that was foolish. What were the chances I'd be able to see Sal alone, to even find her without Mrs Sweet spotting me and making another scene? In my heart of hearts, with an adamant but resigned certainty that seemed almost to have slipped and settled there through the whisperings of a voice outside my own head, I knew I would never see Sal again. Beyond that, I could only imagine the horror on her face if she ever learnt I was secretly part of a cult that worshipped a skull in a shrine and took part in secret rites in a hidden cove; deeds without a name. Then the angry voice came back more strongly and that was definitely my own. The angry voice told me to drive up to Beach View not to see Sal but to face up to Mrs Sweet and make a scene myself. But I knew that was foolish too.

What I needed was to plan. To decide what to do. To make the best out of this mess.

I lay on my back on the narrow bed and stared up at the slanting ceiling of my attic room. A spider was awake too, I saw, but she was ignoring me and weaving her web in the vaulted arch of the dormer gable above the window, over the desk on which my typewriter still stood since I'd typed my letter. I thought of getting up and maybe trying to type something of the book I'd not quite given up starting. But I didn't. I watched the little spider spin her silver threads in the shadows for a while longer, then I got up and instead typed the words I'd heard in my dream, although the arcane symbols I'd seen were beyond my power to replicate. Then I felt calm. I looked at the lines, perfect on the page. *We can both spin a line, little spider*, I thought, *in our own ways*. I dressed and went downstairs to put the kettle on.

I was making a pot of tea, listening to the changing sounds of the kettle as it boiled. It was an electric kettle, but an old one, I admired its rounded shape, all chrome and shiny but pitted in places with spots of rust, and its smooth black Bakelite handle and protruding socket at the back. The word 'Swan' was etched into the side of the chrome, and the spout was long and curved like a swan's neck. I watched the spout for steam rising and thought of swans moving with grace on the surface of a lake while paddling furiously through the murk below. In the still otherwise silent house I could hear the slight changes in sound in the Swan's round belly as the water started to boil and bubble within.

When the sound became loud and steam rose in clouds of white vapour, misting the window, I knew I had to turn the kettle off at the wall. I guess it was faulty, not having some inner mechanism to make it stop, but none of us could afford the expense of a new one and in any case I found the routine soothing – the listening and watching and waiting for the precise moment to stop the power and pull the plug. It was a kind of ritual itself. I poured a little boiled water into the teapot to warm it, poured that out and spooned in enough loose-leaf tea for the pot. All part of the ritual. It was English Breakfast this time, nice and strong. I was the only one who used loose-leaf tea. The others thought I was strange and stuck to bags. But the familiar pattern of actions and result were calming. I enjoyed the quiet time to complete the rite without interruption, and I knew how I liked my tea.

I was pouring myself my first cup when I was surprised by a knock at the door to the flat. It was Asher, looking like he hadn't slept too much either. Looking like he'd just pulled on the same clothes he'd probably been wearing the night before for his comedy routine: bright parachute pants and a baggy shirt covered in a garish print of eyes behind bars. They were crumpled and stained.

"Are you okay?" I asked.

He hesitated on the doorstep. "Yeah. Well, sort of. Are you okay though? Can I come in and chat? I mean, if you're okay with that?"

"Sure, come in. I've made tea. D'you want some?" I decided I didn't mind the interruption. Finding out if Baz had said anything, and if so what, was important.

"Yeah, yeah. Ta, thanks." Asher came into the flat, his eyes darting around nervously.

I poured tea for us both. There was an awkward silence. Asher perched on the edge of the sofa and cleared a space in the random junk on the table for his mug. I sat down in the saggy green armchair with my own.

"Are you okay?" he asked again. Obviously he must know something about what had happened and I suddenly felt anxious. I didn't know what Baz had heard. What might Mrs Sweet have told him? I needed to find out urgently. This mattered.

"Yes, I'm okay. I'll live. What did you hear? What did Baz tell you?"

"He's in a foul temper. Or at least he was last night." Asher looked down sourly, but went on, "Baz got back really late and he really killed the mood. He was angry. Everyone was down in our flat – I mean Jo and Zoe and me. It was a good night at the Lion and we realised you'd got back early and thought you'd gone to sleep and we didn't want to disturb you so we were in our front room, listening to music and having a laugh and so on. Then Baz came in. He looked furious. You could see it on his face. So Jo asked him what was wrong and he scowled and muttered something about you getting the sack because you were an idiot... Shit! ...erm, I don't think that. I don't think you're an idiot at all. Sorry I shouldn't have repeated what he said. Anyway, he told us Mrs Sweet was mad at you and he'd had to step in to help at the bar at the last minute, so he'd not been able to get away to join us at the Lion, and he was pissed off. Then he picked up an empty wineglass and hurled it at the wall so hard it left a dent as well as showering us all with the broken bits. We were all really fucking shocked and I was pretty scared. Honest. I've not seen him like that. Not often. Then he stormed out of the house again and we just stared at each other, kinda stunned. We didn't know what to do. We were pretty wasted. Anyway, we went out to look for him, up and down the seafront, but couldn't find him so eventually we all came back. Then we saw his bike was gone, so he could have gone anywhere. I don't think he's back now either, but I don't know for sure. Sometimes he chains his bike up outside. I didn't sleep much, but if he came back he might be there, sleeping. Can I stay up here for a while? And can you tell me what really happened?"

I don't think I'd ever heard Asher say quite so much in one go except when he was on stage. He was plainly shaken. It didn't seem Baz had given much away, but I still didn't know what Baz thought was going on. Oddly, I felt slightly calmer. If Baz hadn't said anything important, I could tell my side of it first. Asher and Jo and Zoe would understand; be on my side. I was angry with Baz and I was worried and still very angry, but it was colder anger. It was the kind for plotting, and they say revenge is sweet. I took a sip of tea before replying.

"Yes. I can tell you what happened. I kissed a girl and the boss saw and was vile about it. She sacked me coz she's a bitch like that. I guess she took it out on Baz too. But if he thinks I'm the one in the wrong, he can keep out of my way. You can tell him that if you see him."

Asher's eyes looked wider than the ones on his shirt as he spoke his mind on the matter. "I don't even want to see him until I know he isn't going to throw any more stuff around. In fact, after what you told me, I don't think I want to see him at all. Perhaps I could move in up here – sleep in that creepy little attic room that's supposed to be Zoe's?"

Although he wasn't smiling, I knew he was joking at that last comment. He meant the room opposite mine; colder, damper, darker and more full of spiders. Officially it was Zoe's, but all she kept there were some spare clothes and her art stuff. Apart from that it was just a box room with a tiny, unused bed. You'd have to be desperate to consider moving in there.

"Okay, no need to be my go-between. You don't even have to tell him you've seen me," I replied. "Thanks for coming to see me and ask how I was though. I appreciate it. And I'm glad you had a good night at the Lion. I'm sorry I missed it. Would have been better if I'd skipped work, phoned in sick and come with you all last night. But I didn't, and that's that. You can stay up here if you want as far as I'm concerned, if you don't want to see Baz yet."

Jo emerged from the room she shared with Zoe. It was the big warm room on this floor, not the box room in the attic. The sound of us talking must have woken her. She looked half asleep still and was wearing her pyjamas which looked as dishevelled as Asher's clothing, but she came straight over and was full of sympathy.

"Do you want to tell me exactly what happened, or would you prefer not to?"

"It's okay," I said, and I started to tell the fuller story. And Zoe came out too and listened.

"I'm so sorry. That's incredibly unfair," said Jo, when I'd finished. "Do you want a hug?"

"Yes," I said. I did. And she gave me a hug, and so did Zoe, and Asher. And I had all the care I could hope for. It felt good – whatever Baz thought about it. He could get in the sea as far as I was concerned. We talked it over further, Jo, Zoe, Asher, and me.

"I'm not sure there's much you can do about it legally," said Jo, when we'd discussed it in detail. "You hadn't been there long enough to go to an employment tribunal. I wish I could think of something we could do to help. It really sucks. It's completely unfair."

"Honestly, you are helping, just by being here and listening," I said. I'd already realised there was little I could do about my treatment legally. It would be my word against Mrs Sweet's even if I had been there ages. In any case the job did suck and I was best off out of it. Better looking at that job advert my mum was sending me. I told them about that and they agreed. But my plan was coming together in my mind, my little revenge, and I didn't tell them about that. I was going to get justice of some kind and I knew how to get it.

I was in the phone box by the harbour armed with enough coins for longer than I'd need. I dialled the number and Mrs Sweet answered.

"Beach View Holiday Camp."

"Hello Mrs Sweet. This is Alison."

There was a pause before Mrs Sweet replied, in her most business-like voice, but I could sense the tension in it.

"Hello Alison. How can I help you?"

"Well, Mrs Sweet, I'm sure you're aware that even under the terms of my temporary contract I'm entitled to a week's pay in lieu of notice."

There was a pause. I imagined she was looking around to see who was in earshot before replying.

"Not in cases of gross misconduct, Alison." She spoke quietly, practically a whisper, but I could almost smell the bile on her breath.

"Ah, I see, gross misconduct. Why are you whispering, Mrs Sweet? Is there someone you don't want to hear this discussion – about misconduct? Should I take the matter to Mr Sweet then? A full discussion of…misconduct? I could type a letter if you like, maybe even an anonymous one?"

She wasn't stupid. She knew what I was threatening. Yes, sure, I was landing Baz in it too, maybe, but after what Asher had told me Baz had said and done, I didn't care that much. Friends are supposed to stick up for each other, aren't they? Not call them idiots and throw stuff at walls and lick the boss's arse when their friends are sacked. The others were on my side. That I was sure of.

"I understand," said Mrs Sweet, after a long pause, still business-like but icy. "All right. I'll send you a cheque."

"I need a reference too," I added. "Don't worry, you won't be likely to see much more of me. I'm applying for a job a long way from here. Write me a reference – a good one – and I'll be out of your hair and gone."

I heard an intake of breath from the other end of the phone and then there was another pause before she spoke again, much louder than before, still business-like but dripping with fake sincerity. I could guess what had happened and I smiled. I doubt she was smiling though.

"Of course I'll be doing that. Hope things work out better for you in future, Alison. Goodbye." Then a click and a dead line. I'll admit I felt slightly guilty. But not much.

The next day the cheque arrived, as did a letter from my mother with the advert for the job on the newspaper. I sat at my little desk with the sunlight shining through the motes of dust on my window and the sparkling web stretching across the vaulted arch inside it, warming my fingers as I fed a fresh sheet of paper into my typewriter and started my application. The words came smoothly: qualifications, past experience, reasons I so wanted this perfect job. Then the references...

"Rosmorta, help me," I whispered as I depressed the keys, tapping out 'Mrs Susan Sweet'.

Chapter 11

The Living Daylights

It must have happened during the night, but I only discovered the damage late the next morning. Jo, Zoe and I had been going to drive up to Charlie's. That was when I saw Emily's windscreen was smashed. It was deliberate, too, of that I was in no doubt. On the driver's seat, among the shattered glass, was a stone. It was dark grey, a hard, flattish, smooth oval. The perfect kind for throwing. No shortage of stones like that on the beach, of course.

Shock turned to tears, turned to anger. Of course Baz had done it, the bastard, and Suzie Sweet, the bitch, was orchestrating it. That was my immediate suspicion at least. I must have said it aloud, because the next thing I knew Jo was saying that I didn't know that for sure.

"It could've just been a random attack, or kids, or someone looking for things to steal. Even if it was Mrs Sweet behind it, it wasn't necessarily Baz who did it. Look, I know it seems odd that we don't know where he is, or what he was thinking or doing. But we shouldn't accuse him without knowing the whole story."

Jo was always so reasonable and I knew she had a point. Asher came out of the house after hearing the commotion and insisted he was certain Baz wouldn't do that. Not to one of us, even if he had thrown a glass at the wall. But Asher didn't look as sure as his words. I cried, and was angry too, and Jo and Zoe gave me a hug again, and I calmed down a bit.

"Yes, of course, I know it wasn't necessarily Baz," I agreed at last. At least, I should have known that, but something was wrong, something was off, something was out of kilter and had been for a while. And we really didn't know where Baz was, at least not for certain, although we were all pretty sure he was staying up at Beach View.

Baz hadn't come back for a few days, ever since that night he'd chucked the glass at the wall and stormed out, taking his bicycle but not much else. We were all worried about him, but none of us wanted to risk going to look for him up at the caravan site. Was he still angry at us? Was he angry at me? Had he decided to pitch in with the Sweets for good? Surely not that, but I was beginning to wonder.

One of the reasons we'd been going up to see Charlie that morning was to find out if she'd heard anything more. Asher had decided to stay behind to wait in case Baz returned when I was out. It was possible Baz was just avoiding me and would sneak home to Mill Lane when I was away. We'd all been to Charlie's cottage the evening before, but she hadn't seen him or heard from him then. We'd stayed until late for an assignation with Rosmorta. It'd been a week since I'd last sat around the table in our little Cult of the Skull and I felt I'd been remiss. That was Sal's fault, of course, but now I was back it felt right to be renewing that practice, raising our glasses to the Bone Mother, our Mother of the Cup of Life and the one who decrees when it is empty. But Baz hadn't been there for quite a while, longer than my absence.

Surveying the mess in and around my car more calmly and listening to the others, I couldn't really think that Baz would do this. Would he? I checked to see if anything had been stolen from Emily. It hadn't, but then I didn't keep anything worth stealing there. I shook tiny bits of glass out of the sleeping bag that lived on the back seat. No one would want to nick that. The ice-scraper was still on the parcel shelf along with an empty cigarette pack that Baz had chucked there last time I gave him a lift to Beach View. I felt disgust at seeing it now. Looking further, my map book was still tucked under the driver's seat where I kept it and nothing was amiss behind the flap of the tiny glove compartment. I used the ice-scraper to sweep more of the tiny shards from the seats, shelf and dashboard. Zoe went back inside and came out with a dustpan and brush. Between us all we swept the car and pavement clean of fragmented glass. All that was left was the pebble, dark and smooth. As I picked it up I felt a tingle of recognition, like déjà vu, like the sensation of it lying in my hand was so familiar, yet I didn't really think it could be. I slipped the stone into the pocket of my jacket, meaning to look at it more later, then shook the feeling off; there were still more practical things to do.

I drove the two miles up to Charlie's place cautiously with Jo sitting next to me and Zoe on the tiny back seat. Without a windscreen the air buffeted our faces and blew our hair into tangles, but there was no way I was going to walk up the steep road and past the caravan park, giving Mr or Mrs Sweet a chance to see me, or me to see them. I wanted to get past that as fast as possible – broken windscreen taken into consideration. I parked up by the stones blocking the road as usual. There was even more importance in visiting Charlie now. If anyone knew how I could get Emily fixed cheaply it would be her.

She did. More than that, she said she'd mend the windscreen for me. Of course she knew of a scrap yard where they'd have an old Morris like Emily that could be broken for spares and wouldn't charge a lot. And she'd fit it for me. It'd be just as it ever was in no time. Before that, she brought out a plastic sheet to tape over the gaping hole to stop any rain getting in and a chain and padlock to stop opportune thieves taking advantage. On top of it all, she offered tea and sympathy and we sat around her warped driftwood table sipping from those cups with sailing ships, and all the world was right again, mostly. We still had the problem of Baz.

Jo was frowning. "I'm worried about him. I mean, I know he sometimes stays over at the caravan park, but it's been days and nights now. You'd think he'd come back to get clothes. And seeing as he stormed out in a temper..."

"It isn't like him to stay away this long," agreed Zoe.

"I'm still not convinced he didn't smash my windscreen," I said.

Jo merely confirmed things she'd said earlier. "I honestly wouldn't have thought that of him even though I know he can act rashly. I could believe it if he'd done it straight after hurling the wineglass, but this was much later. I don't want to judge him in his absence. But you can never tell, so we need to be careful."

Zoe agreed: "No, you can't ever tell. How far can we be sure of anyone entirely, especially any bloke?"

"I don't trust Baz anymore." I wasn't feeling happy, but it was true.

"So we need to do something about that then, don't we?" said Charlie.

I looked at her curiously. "What do you mean?"

"Well, practically, we'll do what we can to prevent more attacks on your car. When the windscreen's fixed I suggest you park her somewhere a few streets away, where no one knows but you. Whether it was Baz or someone else that should keep her out of sight and out of mind."

I nodded at Charlie's sensible suggestion, but she went on.

"Part of the worry's not knowing where he is. I mean, we're all saying we assume he's at the caravan site. He might be. He probably is. But we're all wondering if that isn't so, aren't we? I mean, there's always the possibility he went off on his own on his bike and had an accident. That he's lying in a pit or ditch somewhere. Even dead." As Charlie spoke the words, we all nodded. It was the thing no one else had wanted to say out loud.

"There are two ways we can tackle this. There's the straightforward way. We can just go to Beach View and ask for him or someone phones and asks after him. Asher would probably be the person to do that in the circumstances, but he's not here to ask and the nearest phone box is halfway down the hill. The other way, well, that's to divine where he is with a pendulum. That we could do right now if you've still got that map book, Alice?"

We looked at each other and I knew before anyone said anything we were in agreement. I went to the car and fetched the map. When I got back to the cottage they were getting set up. The cups had been cleared and Rosmorta was with us. Her skull sat at the head of the table. Charlie was whittling a piece of whitish wood into a shape like an inverted teardrop. She attached a short chain to the rounded top, then held the end links between her thumb and forefinger. It slowly began to swing backwards and forwards and then in a circle. I opened the map at the pages showing the road from here to town, the cliffs and the woods. Placing it on the table, I weighted the corners down so the book lay flat. The little X was still there, I noticed, where we'd marked it. It was the first time since that night that I'd looked at those pages and the memories of exhuming the skull flooded back. For a second I thought the empty eye sockets in the bony face were staring there too. Perhaps tonight I'd make another mark and I wondered what it would signify. My heart started to beat faster and my hands were shaking as I lifted them away from the tome.

We dowsed over the map, or rather Charlie did, pinching the chain tight. The pendulum swung in a way that was almost hypnotic, seeming to take a life of its own as it moved backwards and forwards, leading Charlie's arm across the symbolic landscape of the chart to a place not that far away. Then from backwards and forwards the pendulum started going round and round, and then lower, into a tight circle and we all knew where Baz was before Charlie spoke.

"He's at Beach View."

We all breathed a sigh of relief. Then someone asked if we could do a spell to call him to us. I can't remember who it was posed the question, but we were psyched up and in the mood for magic and were all nodding and agreeing. If we could do a spell to call him to come to us, rather than any of us go to find him, that would put our minds at rest. It would mean we wouldn't have to venture among the caravans ourselves.

"Yes," said Charlie, thoughtfully, after a while. "We can try that. I can think of a way. Do you have something that belongs to him?"

I remembered the cigarette packet on Emily's parcel shelf and Charlie said that would do so I fetched it. Then Charlie set to work, opening up the empty carton that still smelled of tobacco and reminded me of Baz lighting up in the car on an easy day back in the hazy perfect time of high summer. But my reverie was broken by Charlie asking if anyone wanted to do the honours of cutting out a little shape of a man. Zoe offered. With the skill of an artist she snipped at the card in neat and precise cuts, and we soon had a miniature figure, an effigy. It even looked a bit like Baz, from his short spiky hair to his narrow jeans and baseball boots, even though it was just an outline, flat and stylised. We were all impressed.

"I want you to all think of Baz," said Charlie. "I want you all to visualise him, picture him clearly in your thoughts, and ask him to come to us."

She lit a small candle and placed it on the map where the lines and contours corresponded to her cottage. She then held the little cardboard figure at the spot where the pendulum had circled and slowly started walking him towards the light.

"Baz, come to us," she intoned, and we all joined in, chanting it over and over. "Come to us. Come to us. Baz, come to us…"

I wondered what would happen with the cardboard man when he reached the candle. Would Charlie put him in the flame? Burn him to pieces? But she didn't. She laid him flat and placed the metal candle holder on top of him, gently.

"Now we can stop calling. The spell's done and we can wait."

"How long?" asked Jo.

"Spells don't always work quickly," Charlie replied. "Some take their time. If Baz is busy doing other things then he isn't going to drop everything straight away and march over here. He'll just feel the call to come, and he will, unless he really doesn't want to. It isn't like we've turned him into some kind of zombie who's going to do everything we wish. I suggest we thank Rosmorta, then make another pot of tea."

We did that, and the candle burnt down, and I closed my map book with the little man sandwiched in place inside it. As we waited, the sky clouded over outside the window, the wind picked up and rattled at the panes. I started to wonder at what we'd really done. I remembered the tale by William Jacobs and half hoped nothing would come of our little wish, but said nothing about that to the others. We waited quite some time. I'm not sure how long. Time seems to stretch oddly when strange things are happening, but it was long enough that I'd started to tell myself he wouldn't come. It wouldn't take that long to cycle from Beach View to the cottage, surely? But then the sound of the wind dropped and I heard footsteps approaching, from behind the cottage. At least I think it was me who first heard them and told the others to listen too. The rest of my thoughts I kept to myself though: *Why is Baz walking? Why is he on foot? Why isn't he on his bike? What if he was dead? What was outside at the door?*

A quiet knock sounded on the wood. None of us answered. I think we all held our breath. There was a second knock and a third. Charlie broke the stillness of our tableaux around the table, and got up to let him in.

Chapter 12

Toy Boy

Charlie opened the door and Baz was standing in the frame, a silhouette against the bright outside daylight. Those of us seated around the table turned and stared, trying to make out his expression and not knowing quite what to say. Charlie broke the silence.

"Hello Baz, you'd better come inside, then you can tell us what's been happening."

Baz came in, stooping under Charlies wooden carvings and general flotsam hanging from the ceiling, and sat down at the table. He seemed okay, but there was something strange about him I felt. Not that I could see anything I'd be able to point out that was odd, it was just a sensation. Or maybe it was that he looked at everyone else around the table but couldn't seem to look me in the eyes. Yes, that was probably it. In one way I was glad if he felt uncomfortable, but in another I was apprehensive.

"I really hoped I'd find you all here," he said, still not looking at me. "It's been really fucking crazy at the caravans. They asked me to stay there until they get more staff. I wanted to let you know."

"Serve 'em right; shouldn't have sacked me." I stared at Baz defiantly. He looked up at that, caught my gaze briefly, then looked down.

"Yeah, I know," he muttered. "The Sweets think they're a law to themselves. Big fish in their own little pool. Thing is they sort of are and there's nothing much anyone's going to be able to do about it."

"Why didn't you cycle here?" I asked, wanting to change the subject but also wondering why he'd been on foot.

"I just felt like walking, I don't know why really, but the route through the woods is the shortest path from there to here. It was nice to get away, stretch my legs and clear my head and think what to say, without thinking about traffic on the road or anything, but really, I'm just sorry. I'm sorry I was in angry. I wasn't angry at you, just angry at what had happened, and I'd had too much to drink. I'm sorry about the broken glass and dent in the wall. I'll fix any damage when I get back, if that's necessary. Should be back tomorrow, or the day after. Can you tell Asher?"

"I'll tell Asher. He's been worried," said Jo.

"Tell him I'm sorry, can you?"

I noticed he still hadn't quite said he was sorry to me. He didn't stay long. He said he had to get back to open the bar. I guess he did.

"Did we really summon Baz here?" Jo asked, when Baz was gone and well out of earshot. It was the question I'd been thinking too.

"Maybe, maybe not," replied Charlie. "That's the way magic works, if it works. Like it could all be coincidence. But who knows? And does it matter? At least we know he's okay."

He might be okay, but I wasn't, and other things weren't, I thought. And I knew I'd have to do something else to make them better.

My windscreen still hadn't been fixed that evening, although Charlie said she'd do it the next day, so I drove back to Mill Lane carefully. I took the sleeping bag and map book and anything else that could get wet in Emily up to my room. When I put the book down it fell open at the same pages as earlier and there was the cardboard cut-out. Then I knew what it was I could do.

I took the cardboard figure of Baz and placed it next to my typewriter, then I threaded a fresh sheet of paper through the rollers and began to type just above the centre of the page. I started with his name, but the rest of the words came as my fingers kept tapping, depressing the keys automatically. Words appeared almost before I was conscious of them:

Baz be nice
and Baz be kind
Baz do what
is on my mind.

That was good, I felt, and I wound the page out. I placed the effigy over the words and folded the paper round it: top third down, bottom third up, one side folded into the folds of the other. A neat package. *That's not quite enough*, whispered a voice inside my head that I had come to recognise and trust. *Take a strand of hair, your hair, and spider silk, that's right. Wind it round three times and tie a knot. Repeat the words, and again, and again. That's done, that's spun, keep it secret, keep it safe...* I tucked the little bundle under my pillow before I went to bed.

I dreamt, and it seemed I woke at the sensation of something climbing onto the foot of my bed. It was perhaps the size of a cat or a small dog and the same weight. I could feel the mattress depress slightly under its footfalls, the indentations of its feet as it moved closer and closer to me. I felt it press against my legs as it folded its own, then seem to settle its body and curl against me as though wanting warmth on a cold night. The air outside the bed did feel cold. There was a chill on my face and any exposed flesh despite it being a summer night. And the creature pressed closer. It was almost as though it purred, although I didn't hear anything. All was silent. But I could feel the purr like a gentle vibration emanating from the body of whatever it was pressed against me.

I wasn't scared. Tucked inside my warm bed, in my little attic room, what had I to be scared of in someone's pet, however mysterious it might be that it had got into the house and into my room? But after a while the mysteriousness of it all grew stronger or, perhaps, I woke more fully to the strangeness of the situation. My body felt heavy with sleep and it was only with great effort that I managed to raise my head from the pillow and turn to see what was there. My eyes met eight others, watching me from a single hairy face; a face fused into a large, rounded, hairy body, and beyond that an even grosser ovaloid abdomen, also covered in long hair. The creature had eight legs attached to its body, all curled up and pressing against my own legs at the foot of the bed.

I tried to scream, but no sound would come from my mouth however wide I opened my jaws and however hard I tried to force air from my lungs to work my vocal cords. No part of my body seemed able to obey my desire to pull back from the creature, to jump out of the bed and run out of the room, to scream and raise everyone in the house and warn them about this monstrous thing. All I could do was tilt my head a tiny, tiny bit and open my mouth in a silent cry.

It was the creature who broke the silence. She chittered quietly as she stared at me. But she didn't move and I forced myself to calm down as best I could. What real difference did it make if this was some huge spider rather than a cat or a dog seeking warmth and comfort on a cold night? And as I calmed, I felt the creature's noiseless purrs again and I knew she meant me no harm. Sometimes we have to take all the companionship we can get, and friends come in all shapes and sizes. One shouldn't judge by appearances.

At length, I regained some movement of my limbs although I still felt sluggish and it was a great effort to move, but I managed to sit up in the bed. The spider didn't move, but continued to watch me with her eight eyes. Cautiously, I reached out, down the bed, with my hand, as I would to a familiar pet, and gently touched the spider's head then stroked her hair. It was soft and velvety to the touch and her head and body felt warm too. She chittered slightly and the purring grew.

"What do you want?" I asked, only realising as I said the words that my powers of speech had been freed.

The spider chittered again, slowly unfurled her legs. She climbed off the bed then slowly moved towards the door.

"Do you want me to open the door?"

The chittering sound seemed to me to indicate that she did, although I'm not sure why I should have thought that. I got out of the bed and put on my dressing gown, then opened the door for the spider. She walked out in that strange way that spiders move, alternating pairs of her legs with two pairs in the air and two pairs on the ground, then the ones on the ground raising and those in the air lowering in a way that was difficult for human eyes to take in. She moved out of the door in that fashion and across the tiny landing to the other door on the far side, the one to the box room that was never usually opened. But the spider stopped before it and chittered again as if asking me to open that too. So I did. I turned the handle and pushed, and the door creaked loudly, as doors that are rarely opened can do in old houses in the dead of night. The creature skittered forwards into darkness. I did not follow.

I woke and it was morning. The sun was streaming in through my window and I could hear other people in the house. Raised voices. It sounded as though Jo and Zoe were having a row. I couldn't quite make out all the words but it seemed to be something about a painting. Although I was desperate for a cup of tea, I didn't want to go downstairs into the middle of an argument, so I put on my dressing gown and wondered what to do until the angry voices subsided. Then I remembered my dream, and it made me curious about what was in the room opposite my own. I hadn't spent any time there. No one did, or so I thought. I mean, we all knew it was officially Zoe's room, but she didn't sleep there.

Carefully I tiptoed across the bare boards of the upper landing and turned the handle of the door opposite mine, just as I recalled doing in my sleep the night before but without a giant spider at my feet. The door opened. Inside, everything was pretty much as I remembered it from the previous time I'd glimpsed inside. Although the curtains were pulled back, little light crept in. The narrow window faced the wrong side of the house and the old glass was thick with grime. Boxes stood in a stack to one side and by the other was the narrow bed.

But there were a few things I'm sure hadn't been there last time I'd looked. I knew Zoe used this room to store some of her art stuff, but there was a sketchbook on the bed and leaning next to it was a canvass covered in a cloth. Zoe must have been busy without me realising it, when I was working or out with Sal or otherwise not around. I lifted the cover of the sketchbook. Staring out at me was the face of a spider, filling the page. I probably gasped. I turned over the page and there were more spiders and bones too, and the skull. This was distinctly different from what I'd seen of Zoe's earlier stuff – that had been local scenes, beachscapes and landscapes, things she was hoping might sell to tourists and the like. These were something poles apart. I wasn't surprised at the pictures of the bones, and I guessed I wasn't the only one dreaming of spiders.

Then I lifted the cloth covering the canvas. It was a painting, in oils, but this one was different again. It was a face I recognised, but she was clearly dead. In that instant I realised what the argument I'd heard had been about. I put the cloth back over the picture, left the room and closed the door behind me. Perhaps Jo and Zoe had heard me moving upstairs because the sounds of their disagreement had stopped. I went down to the living room and they both acted as if nothing was wrong.

"Morning. Do you want a cup of tea?" asked Zoe.

"Thanks." I tried to force normality into my voice and faked a smile.

"Some post's come for you," said Jo, thrusting an envelope into my hand. I opened it. It seemed I'd got that interview. Well, there was a thing. I told the others and they congratulated me. I still wasn't really sure this was what I wanted, but I certainly wasn't going to turn it down. I smiled again, without needing to fake it this time.

"I guess we need to celebrate then," I said.

"Definitely!" said Jo, with a huge smile too.

"A party on the beach?" Zoe suggested.

And that was what we decided to hold.

Chapter 13

Live It Up

"I wish we'd never found those horrible bones, or we'd left them to fall in the sea," said Asher, vehemently.

We were on the beach, the secret beach, for the party. We'd carried most of what we needed around with us at low tide. The sun was setting amid golden clouds beyond the cliffs behind us and the moon was rising over the sea. It was the brightest of evenings. We'd dumped our bags and jackets in a heap and were going to collect driftwood to build a fire, but first we all sat down on the sand, cracked open beers and watched the waves. Zoe and Jo were off to one side, arms around each other. Charlie and Baz seemed deep in discussion, so I sat down next to Asher. Remembering the first time I was on this beach and the wishes I'd made with Jo and Zoe, I asked Asher to make one. He made three wishes in all, and those first two were about the bones.

"Why do you hate the bones so much?" I asked.

He looked down, avoiding my gaze, and paused before answering. "Before we found them, before we dug them up, we just had fun, had a laugh, got drunk, smoked weed. Now everything's creepy and shit."

"But don't you think it would've been bad to let them fall off the cliff and be lost forever?"

"Not really. If they'd been somewhere a long way away from Charlie's place, then sure, I guess. Someone would've dug them up officially and put them in a museum perhaps, but that's creepy too. I'm with Charlie on that one. If someone's buried, they should stay buried, and their bones should crumble like they were meant to."

I partly agreed. "I can see that, but archaeology helps us find out about the past. Old bones can help us to find out where we came from, our ancestors."

"Not my ancestors," said Asher. "Not yours either. Probably none of us are even remotely related to whoever it is we are calling our 'grandmother' now. Charlie knows where her real gran's buried. Jo's family originally came from Nigeria. Baz doesn't talk about his family a lot, but I know pretty much all of us came here to get away from our relatives. I know you're thinking of going home if you get that job, but you don't want to. You hate your parents. I hate my dad. I'm here so I can be myself rather than do what he wants me to do. Similar with Jo and Zoe. Why do you think they have nothing to do with their relatives, even though they don't live that far away? We don't need made-up stuff and I just wish I wasn't part of our little cult of the skull. That's probably what I wish for most." And so Asher made his third and final wish.

"It's Suzie Sweet I blame for things being shit, not the bones," I argued.

"That was harsh, what she did. I can understand you blaming her, but that wasn't really what I was talking about. Look, I think we should just have fun tonight. Get drunk, smoke some weed, have a laugh like we used to. Maybe things'll turn around here. Maybe things'll be different after this."

"Yes." I agreed wholeheartedly to that. We clinked our beer cans and smiled in unison. Then Charlie came up to us.

"We need to start collecting kindling," she said.

We each wandered off in various directions. It was easy to find things to burn on the beach. There was driftwood, some of it natural, some planks or bits of crate or other things that had once served some man-made purpose, all broken and salt-stained. Once dry, sea-changed wood burns well. At the top of the beach there were nearly always a few twigs and branches fallen from the trees on the cliff. After a storm there'd be plenty and there had been a few recently. We'd brought newspaper and some small, dry sticks with us as well as plenty of matches, so we knew we could get a fire going. Other flotsam and jetsam could be burnt too at a pinch, like bits of rope, although more and more of it was plastic these days which you shouldn't burn because it gives off fumes. Jo talked about that as we dumped beachcombed armfuls onto the growing wood pile.

"We ought to collect the plastic too, but take it back with us."

"I know, but we need to concentrate on the firewood first." I looked around. Twilight was darkening and even on a clear night under a full moon it would be less easy to find things on the beach. Once the fire was lit it would seem pitch black outside the flickering circle.

"In the morning, before we leave, after we gather up our own stuff, we should clean the beach, leave it better than we found it, leave nothing but footprints in the sand," said Jo.

"Always best to leave a place better than one finds it," I agreed, but I felt a twinge of guilt. Had I ever left a place better than I found it? Jo and I both wandered off to collect more wood, but found ourselves together again as we returned with more and decided where to start the fire.

"The ideal thing is to dig a hollow below the high tide mark, so the sand below the fire's still wet. The hollow shields the flames and any last embers get put out when the water rises," Jo said. "It stops things smouldering below the surface, spreading and harming anything living in the sand. But if we do that tonight our fire'll go out before dawn. We'll be here longer than that. So, I suggest we build a cairn just below the high tide mark instead and put our fire on top. Then the water should go around it, but not put it out."

As the others returned with more driftwood the idea caught everyone's imaginations and we started to pull together rocks and stones to build a cairn with a bowl-like top to house our fire. But as we did that I was suddenly worried someone would spot the flames and come to try to save us, thinking we were lost or stranded by the tide. I thought of Robinson Crusoe, too scared to have a fire in case it was seen, or the children in *Lord of the Flies* lighting a beacon that turned to wildfire. I shivered and Jo saw me.

"You're cold. We'd better get the fire alight quickly." She handed me one of the blankets from her backpack.

We sat around the fire with more beer cans open. Baz and Asher were vying over what mixtape to put on the boom box, Jo and Zoe were delving into bags trying to find the food we'd brought and Charlie was skinning up. I was sitting next to her watching the beach scene and us preparing things, thinking how perfect it was. It was a still, calm, moonlit night. So peaceful. I knew that would change when the music started, but for the time being I was just enjoying the crackle of the growing fire and the sound of the sea and the gentle murmur of voices.

"What are you thinking?" asked Charlie.

"Just enjoying the moment, really, the peace and quiet, the fact that we have this all to ourselves. I love this beach. I want to remember it just like this."

"I heard you and Jo talking earlier. I agree we should do a beach clean. I could do more with the plastic and metal and glass that's washed up. I've collected bits in the past, but not done much with them except hang some from my ceiling. I should think more and maybe turn them into something like my wooden pieces, only different," Charlie said, then changed the subject. "How's your book going?"

"Not well," I admitted, honestly. "I've not written much. Just poems really. Not a book, not like I intended."

"You will though, one day. You will write your book, and you'll write about us and this beach. Maybe not exactly, but you will." Charlie looked certain and I was a little shocked at her insight. Maybe it showed in my face.

"Here," she said, smiling and handing me the spliff. As I took a toke the sound of This Corrosion echoed around the cove. I guessed who'd won the battle of the mixtapes, and the party was on.

We drank and smoked and danced and stoked the fire. It was a good night then. The tide came in, inexorably of course, and there came a time when the waves broke close and the water flowed into our circle of light. We had to move the blankets and bags and beer and food, and of course the boom box, and there was a mad scramble with shrieks as the waves splashed us and water started to run around the base of our cairn.

"Bank it up!" someone shouted. So we piled sand around the base to protect our heap of stones against the encroaching tide and for a while it worked as the swash flowed around the tower we'd built, but finally it encircled it and waves broke over the rocks and splashed up, spray fizzing and hissing as it met the flames.

"Build up the fire now!" someone called out as we realised we had done all that was possible to stop the tower falling and all we could do was keep the fire alight. So we ran into the water and put more kindling on the cairn top, but at last we had to retreat even from that and just watch and hope our structure would stand, a castle on the beach in a battle of the elements. And it did. And at last the tide turned, and retreated, and our fire smouldered on. We'd won the night. A bottle of rum was opened and passed around to celebrate.

"It's like an altar more than a cairn, isn't it?" muttered Zoe quietly to me, much later in the predawn light. The others had gone off to try to find more kindling, but Zoe had sat down on the blanket next to her bag and got out her sketchbook to draw the scene.

"Yes," I agreed. It kind of was. "An altar to Rosmorta, do you think?" I was trying to find a way to ask Zoe what I'd been wanting to ask her.

"Yes, probably. Definitely. It's all about her now, isn't it? Even when she isn't here," Zoe affirmed that much of what I'd been thinking.

"Yes, yes it is. I saw your pictures of her in your room. I hope you don't mind that I looked. The door was open," I lied.

"That's okay," said Zoe. "I don't sleep there."

"So, what's with the Dorian Gray thing then, if you don't mind me asking?" I wondered if I'd stepped too far.

"Ah, yes..." Zoe paused before going on. "I've been having strange dreams."

"Yeah, me too." I rummaged in the detritus of the party and found the rum. There was still some in the bottle. I took a swig then offered it to Zoe. "I've been dreaming about spiders, mostly."

"Yes, spiders, and the skull, and then I had this dream in which I saw myself. I was looking down and I looked dead. It was so real. I woke up and I had to start painting it. I don't know exactly why, but it felt that if I painted it, if I painted it exactly as I saw it, it would offset the reality. Does that make sense?"

"Yes, it does." I thought of the messages I felt I'd had through dreams, and what I'd done afterwards.

"I'm glad you understand. I'm glad someone does. Jo and I had a row about it. Please don't tell anyone else." She looked worried.

"I won't," I promised. Then I went on. "Look, maybe we should make an offering to Rosmorta? The rest of this rum...?"

"Yes!" Zoe checked the bottle. There was enough. We each took a small last swig, making sure there was still some in it, then went to the fire and poured our libation, emptying the rest and whispering our prayers to Our Lady of the Bones.

In the morning light we did our beach clean. We took carrier bags we'd brought food in and filled them with other old bottles and cans and bits of rope and a mangled flip-flop and other unidentifiable things washed up along the high-water margin. There weren't enough bags for each of us, so Baz asked me to go with him. I was curious to see what he might say.

"Look, I'm sorry," he said when the others were out of earshot. "I really am. I know you think I sided with Suzie over you, but I really didn't."

"Hmmm, it kind of seemed like you did."

"Yeah, I know. I know. I had to. She's dangerous. I've told you. You think you've got one over on her, I know, getting that cheque off her, but she likes to control things, to control people. She's smart, not as smart as you, but she holds grudges."

"So it wasn't you smashed my windscreen?"

"Fuck no!" Baz turned to look me straight in the eyes. "No, I wouldn't do that. She has other lackies. Trust me. Please. I can be your eyes and ears. I'll do whatever you want. I really like you, Alice. I want to help."

"Okay," I said. And Baz smiled, and so did I.

We walked on in silence. Then, on the sand, I found a plastic doll. It was a fashion doll, a famous brand or some cheap copy. There was something about her black hair and bright red lips that made me shudder. I looked at Baz and I could see we thought the same thing. I was about to shove the thing into the rest of the rubbish when I had another idea. I gave Baz the bag and ran to the cairn with the embers still burning and held her over.

"What are you doing? You can't burn plastic!" Jo shouted.

The others turned to look at what I was doing, gathering close. I could see a mix of feelings on their faces beyond Jo's disapproval, from curiosity to fascination to just a little fear.

Only in Baz's eyes was there understanding but I surprised myself at how strongly I felt about it.

"I'm doing this. The bitch can burn."

I dropped her into the fire, but she didn't start to smoulder immediately. I guess dolls are flame retardant, but after a few moments her hair and clothes were wreathed in small blue flames, then the plastic started to shrink and fold in on itself, giving the impression it was writhing. The face went last, those big eyes in pale, pale cheeks, and for a moment I felt like pulling the doll out, but really there was no way to do that safely, and the mouth sucked in one last time. I watched the sunken pile of wood with the effigy melting in the flames. And the time ran on, and the wind started to rise. As the little woman shrivelled and shrunk words came to me from a Rossetti poem, though I think I remembered it wrong: *'If now it be molten, all is well... What more to see, between Heaven and Hell?'*

Of course, our packing took longer than expected and we weren't quite as scrupulous as we had hoped. It was a rush to finish before the tide turned again. We were a subdued group that trudged our way around the headland. Dark clouds had formed in the sky, covering the sun, and the wind was high. We made it though, and at last we were home to a little sleep.

Chapter 14

Wipeout

I woke to the sounds of the wind and the rain outside and raised voices in the room below. It sounded different to the row I now knew was about Zoe's painting, so I put on my dressing gown and stumbled downstairs, hungover, still half asleep. Jo and Zoe also looked half asleep and were watching Asher rummage in the bags of debris we'd brought back from the beach.

"It has to be here somewhere here!" Asher shouted as he threw old bottles and other detritus out of a rubbish bag in a frantic search for something.

"What're you looking for?" I asked.

"My mixtape!" He looked up at me, as though accusing me of taking it. I hadn't, of course, I didn't even remember seeing it. I'd not paid much attention to exactly what had been put on the boom box, although I did recall Asher's mix of house and other dance tracks had played after Baz's rock and goth tape. It was shorter though. I think we only heard one side before there was a change again. I couldn't remember exactly what came on in what order. I tried to think back but all I could recollect was that Jo's Diamond Life cassette was playing after the battle of the fire cairn, when we were chilling. I remembered seeing Jo and Zoe dancing soulfully to Your Love is King, and wishing Sal was there. That wasn't much help though.

Jo asked: "Are you absolutely sure you've searched well enough in your own things?"

"Yes, I've gone through everything; mine and Baz's bags. Twice," he insisted.

"I'll look in my bag," said Zoe and disappeared back into the main bedroom.

I put the kettle on. Jo helped Asher search through the remaining bits and pieces we'd brought from the beach, then put all the rubbish back into the bags it came out of. Asher looked defeated by the time the tea was made. He sipped morosely.

"Look, I know you don't want to lose the tape, but if you can't find it, can you just make another with the same stuff on it?" I asked.

Asher sighed. "No. No, I can't. There was music on one side and I can tape that again, but the other side was a recording of my best ever live set. A private gig. It went so well. I improvised jokes and everyone laughed. Normally I have to work so hard, but that night it was like I'd always dreamed of being when I'm on stage. I really need that recording. I don't know what I'd do if I lost it. I mean, it would be gone for good, forever. There's no others."

I nodded. I understood. As a writer, sometimes you get an idea for a short story or poem or something and you know it's brilliant, but you have to write it down straight away or the idea will be gone. For some it's worse. Jilly Cooper left the only copy of her manuscript for *Riders* on a bus. It was never found again. She was so upset she didn't even try rewriting the novel for about 15 years. But although I understood why Asher was upset, I couldn't understand why he'd taken something that precious to the beach. Jo must have had the same thoughts.

She asked: "Why d'you bring it to the party, Asher?"

"I dunno. Well, I mean, apart from wanting to play my mixtape, of course," he said. But I suddenly realised it was more than that. I think he'd been hoping to play his comedy set too, but had chickened from putting it on. Now he was probably even more offended that we didn't realise he'd wanted to wow us with his gags. And it was gone. Maybe. I didn't feel we should give up hope yet. I suggested another search of every box and bag, and all our pockets too. So we did that, but still no luck.

Asher looked at his watch. "I'm going back to the beach to search. It'll be low tide again in a couple of hours. Maybe it'll be there still, above the tideline."

"You can't do that," said Jo, looking towards the window against which rain was hammering. "The weather's much too bad. But when it eases, maybe next tide, we'll all go. If it's there it'll still be there later. No one else'll be able to get there before us."

"Okay," muttered Asher, but he still looked unhappy.

"We could ask Rosmorta to help," I suggested, thinking it might be at least something we could do.

Asher wasn't having that. "No way. No way. I'm sick to death of Rosmorta this, Rosmorta that. Can't we just forget all that shit? I've had enough of her. I'm done with her. I think we should just chuck that skull and bones into the sea and all have done with her too. Especially after this!"

"Oh," I said, noncommittally.

It was Jo who gave a voice of reason again. "It isn't really up to us, is it? Charlie found the bones and she's still got them. You'd need to discuss it with her, but I do want us all to be happy. How about we discuss it later, after we've found your tape?"

"Okay," said Asher, but he looked away and wouldn't meet anyone's eyes.

After he'd left the flat and gone downstairs, I rummaged around in the cupboard under the kitchen sink and found matches and a candle we had in case of power cuts. It was just a stub in an old brass holder with a little handle coated in ancient wax drips, but it would do. I took it back up to my room where I put it on my table, lit it and knelt in front of it like I might a votive flame in a church, but I prayed to Rosmorta.

"Please Rosmorta, please help. Let us find Asher's tape. Please. I promise I'll do whatever you ask in return, but please help with this."

Candlelight flickered around the arch of the window, fluttering in draughts as the wind rattled the frame and found gaps in the old woodwork, but stayed alight. *Do you look for answers when you pray?* I wondered. *Do you look for signs your words have been heard by higher powers?* I heard nothing except the storm raging on outside the house, the rain battering the glass and the wind howling so loudly I was scared it would take the tiles off the roof and let water leak into my little attic room, to drip on my head and soak my few precious things. That didn't happen, although I thought of Asher's mixtape lying on the beach, the rain falling on it where perhaps it had been left. I didn't know whether cassettes would survive that. A book manuscript certainly wouldn't, but I hadn't lost one. I didn't exactly have a manuscript to lose, did I?

After my candle burnt low and eventually spluttered out, I went back downstairs. Jo and Zoe had all the lights on even though it was day and a little portable electric fire in front of the sofa on which they huddled. I sat down in the green chair, staring at the glowing bars and willing the warmth to seep my way. We stayed there without speaking, listening to the storm, until we heard the sounds of footsteps climbing the stairs and the knock at the door. Jo went to open it. Baz was outside.

"Is Asher here?" he asked.

"No. He went downstairs ages ago. Has he found his tape?"

"No, and he isn't there. I wanted to tell him I'd searched my room again. No sign of it though. I was hoping he'd found it here."

"Shit!" Jo turned and looked at our clock on the wall. "He must've gone to the beach. It'll be about low tide now."

"He can't have done, not in this weather," said Zoe.

"Yeah, he can, stupid fucking idiot," said Baz.

Jo turned back to face us, her eyes open wide. "Right, we have to go after him – now! It'd be crazy trying to get round the headland in this weather. We have to go talk some sense into him before he gets that far."

We all agreed, and pulled on boots and coats and jackets and whatever waterproofs we could find and headed out into the gale. We went as quickly as we could, battling our way along the promenade with the wind against us, buffeting us, trying to force us back inland. We could see huge rollers crashing far away down the beach – it was definitely low tide – and there was a figure, a dark silhouette, barely visible against the rolling clouds in the grey sky, tiny in the distance under the looming headland. Our fears confirmed, we hurried onwards.

"Stop! Asher!" shouted Baz, but there was no point. There was no way he could hear us through the storm.

We were forced to slow when we descended the worn, narrow, slippery steps to the shingle, helping each other not to fall. Asher was still ahead of us and hadn't looked round, but I think we were gaining on him. We could still see him picking his way over the foreshore around the curved base of the cliff. We tried to run, but the faster you try to move over pebbles and shingle, the more they slip back underfoot, hampering your progress. It was almost like running in one of those nightmares when you can't seem to get anywhere no matter how hard you try – but not quite.

"We need to stop him before he reaches the rocks." Jo urged us on.

Baz called Asher's name again, we all did, but the wind was against us and our voices, even in unison, failed to carry. The rain was lashing down now and the sky almost black. It seemed as dark as night even though it was day. Suddenly, in a flash of lightning, we saw Asher again, sharply this time, just about to start climbing the rocks this side of the headland. Huge waves were breaking against them just a little further out.

"Stop!" I screamed, but my cry was lost in a boom of thunder, which must have been almost directly overhead. All of us were blinded for a moment by that bright flash, but we carried on as best we could. Slowly our vision of the beach got better, but there was no sign of Asher at all. We never saw him alive again.

We made it to the rocks in the tidal stretch of the beach, green and slippery and even more treacherous than usual. We tried to make it round the headland, but gave up. Really, no sane person would have attempted it. So we turned back and went to the phone box by the harbour where we called the coastguards. There was nothing else we could do. They told us to go home and wait, so that was what we did.

We waited. Later, I don't know how much later, there was a knock at the front door. We all rushed down, crowded into that narrow corridor by the bicycles. Baz got there first. A police officer stood outside. She asked if she could come in. I think for a moment we all instinctively wanted to say, "No, not without a search warrant", but no one did. We all realised she'd come to tell us that a body had been found.

Chapter 15

Heartache

Baz was asked to formally identify the corpse as none of Asher's relatives were in the area. It was him, of course. Asher's death was reported to a coroner, as happens when someone dies unexpectedly. The police asked us all questions about what happened and said there'd be an inquest. There was, but not for a while. Everyone seemed certain the verdict would be death by misadventure. Apparently it's easier to drown in seawater than in fresh water, especially when the weather's cold. Someone reassured us we weren't likely to be considered culpable, but it hanged over us nevertheless. When Asher's father arrived to collect his things, we all felt he blamed us. Hell, we blamed ourselves. But at least the authorities released his body quickly and his father arranged for the funeral, which we were determined to attend even though it was far away.

All of us wore black to the funeral, dressing our smartest. I made sure we arrived not too early and not too late, parking Emily at the far side of the cemetery. We tried to be as respectable and respectful as possible as we quietly stood at the back of the crowd of people we didn't know around the hole in the ground that was to accept the mortal remains of our dear friend. We bowed our heads as an officiant in a religion Asher hadn't believed in said some platitudes that had nothing to do with our memories of the lovely, funny, shy person who had been such an important part of our lives. It all seemed so hollow. I wanted to offer to read a poem, but didn't feel my intrusion would have been welcome so I stayed silent. But, as the man in holy robes asked God for mercy on Asher's soul so he might enter Heaven, I went over in my own mind the other words, the ones I had wanted to say, ones I had read in an article about contested authorship. Some said the poem was by Mary Frye, others by Clare Harner. Whoever wrote it, it was perfect:

> Do not stand at my grave and weep
> I am not there. I do not sleep.
> I am a thousand winds that blow.
> I am the diamond glints on snow.
> I am the sunlight on ripened grain.
> I am the gentle autumn's rain.
> When you awaken in the morning's hush,
> I am the swift uplifting rush
> Of quiet birds in circled flight.
> I am the soft stars that shine at night.
> Do not stand at my grave and cry;
> I am not there. I did not die.

And then it came to me with those unsaid words, that Asher wasn't really dead and gone, not his spirit. If Rosmorta could be with us despite being buried thousands of years ago, so could Asher. We just needed something of him to bring him back. But then the coffin was lowered into the grave and a prayer was said. We tried to join in, quietly, without drawing attention to ourselves even though it felt meaningless. His dad didn't invite us back for sherry and condolent conversation after the funeral, so I drove us all home to Mill Lane.

There, in our familiar flat, we decided to put on music for the first time since that party, in remembrance of Asher. Baz came up with the boom box and a cassette case in his hands. It was Diamond Life. At least, that was what it said on the outside. Inside was Asher's mixtape. It must have been there since the party, put there without thinking, just by mistake. An accident. A tragic, tragic accident.

Chapter 16

So Emotional

I travelled back to my parents' home before my job interview. In some ways I was glad to have a break from the oppressive atmosphere that had grown at Mill Lane. We were all in grief and our grief seemed to feed itself and feed each other's ways of trying to cope with Asher's absence; the hole he left by not being there. There was often silence when we were together. Sometimes silence was better, especially when it was the silence of shared emotion, of not knowing what words to say because words are never enough and won't fill the void, just echo in it meaninglessly. Silence in those circumstances made us closer in our loss, but also more introspective, each trying to find our own way out of the shared darkness. But silence was also better because sometimes the words exchanged weren't kind. This was when I told Zoe the truth about her tea – that I had never liked the way she made it. She let me brew it after that, but I knew I'd hurt her. I was bitchy and wrong. Those kinds of things pushed us apart.

It wasn't always like that though. We'd communed with Rosmorta. It wasn't a séance. None of us felt ready for that. But we had sat around the table with the skull at the head and each in turn said something about Asher – our brightest memories of him. We had asked Rosmorta to guide his spirit wherever spirits went. We raised a toast and also poured a libation into the soil at the top of the cliff. We knew this ritual was something we had to do, but I think all of us secretly also knew it wasn't what Asher would have wanted. I didn't feel easier after that, but I did feel more resolved. I knew I had to get on with my own life and follow my path where fate – and perhaps magic – was leading. So I set off for the interview. But before I left, I went to the edge of the cliff by myself.

I remembered a short horror story by E Nesbit called 'From the Dead'. In it, a woman stands at the top of a cliff and drops a white handkerchief onto the beach below, leading people to think she's jumped. She does die, but much later in complications from childbirth rather than as a result of her own lethal actions. She eventually comes back from the dead too, but the story is more about grief than about dying. It's about the regrets you have and the things you never said but should have and words said in anger that are never forgotten. But also the story is about hope that those once close can hear our words of love and sorrow even after death. I said a few words into the wind but saw no ghosts. Then I walked back to Emily and drove the long drive away.

The interview went well and I felt moderately confident afterwards. The editor said she'd let me know, but she had other people to see. She also told me that head office would need to rubber stamp any appointment too. It could be a while. I stayed a few days at my parents' home, my old home, partly to see how I felt if it was to be my home again. It wasn't great, but I knew by then it was a sacrifice I could make if I needed to. It wouldn't be forever. I promised myself that. Then I drove back to the coast and my friends, and my feelings were mixed.

I'd been away only a short time, but things seemed different at Mill Lane when I returned. Zoe was out when I got back into the flat. Jo told me she'd decided to put more effort into selling her pictures and was spending time out and about with Charlie to draw beach scenes. The woman who managed the shop that sold Charlie's wooden items had agreed to stock some of Zoe's work. She'd even put one watercolour in the window already.

I have to admit I felt a twinge of envy. Why hadn't I put that much effort into my book? But, on the whole, I was pleased for her. Jo said that she'd applied to volunteer at the Samaritans. She wanted to help people. *People like Asher, or people like us?* I wondered. Baz was out too. He'd thrown himself into his role at the caravan park once more and was staying there overnight quite often. Jo said he'd told her he hated to be in his empty flat with Asher's room all cleared out and vacant. He was thinking of moving, he'd admitted, rather than look for another flatmate.

I felt shocked. Of course I was considering moving away too, but Baz? Surely not. Was this how it all ended, with us all going off in our own directions? I went to my room and lay on the little bed and cried. But things did get better. And the thing that brought us back together, at least for a while, was the charity night at the Golden Lion.

It was Baz's idea. He talked to Rick, the pub manager, and suggested they hold an open mic night in memory of Asher and to raise money for the RNLI. The Lifeboat Institution is connected to the Coastguards, but runs as a charity. The volunteers on the local boat might have been too late to stop Asher drowning, but the service saves countless lives at sea each year. It felt good to maybe help rescue others. The publican agreed with a nod and a simple, gruff, "Good idea. We'll do it," and so it was set in motion and we all got involved.

Zoe created a poster and leaflets advertising Take the Mike for Lifeboats – a charity night of comedy and music. Baz had suggested the name. Jo visited the high street printshop and persuaded them to copy the flyers for free. That wasn't the only local business which got behind it. Many did. I got flyers put out at the library and in the newsagent. Pretty much everyone we talked to agreed to put a poster up somewhere – in their window or on a noticeboard or something. Some did more and offered prizes for a raffle or straight out donated money. It felt like the whole town was coming together over this. But not the caravan park. Baz asked, but apparently Suzie felt anything that made holidaymakers think the coast was dangerous was bad for custom. Like we needed any more evidence she was nasty.

I typed a press release and sent it to our local newspaper. As I did so, I wondered why I'd not thought of seeing if they needed an editorial assistant. I'd browsed the section with adverts for jobs each week, of course, but never thought of writing to the paper itself on spec. Not that I was going to do that now. I was rushing down when I heard the post each morning to find out if there was any answer about my ongoing application. To look elsewhere would seem like it was jinxing fate and I didn't want to do that.

The night before Take the Mike, I had another strange dream. I was standing at the beginning of a long flagstone corridor in an old building. I didn't recognise it, but it seemed large and imposing and from another era, with high ceilings and tall windows at one side through which I could see it was night-time. The corridor was all in shadows, unlit except by moonlight, yet at the far end of it a door stood open to a brightly illuminated room. From inside that room I could hear music playing faintly and I could see silhouettes of people dancing. I couldn't see them clearly as they flitted past the open door, which seemed a long, long way away, but it appeared to be a party with sounds of gaiety and laughter mingling with the strains of a tune. In between me and that happy place, in the centre of the long hallway, stood my parents side by side with stern looks on their faces. They appeared tall, as though towering above me, or maybe I was small, no more than a child. I felt lost for what to do or say to get past them as I knew they would try to stop me. So we stood there, the three of us, not moving or speaking for what seemed an age. The moon went behind a cloud and the corridor got gloomier. The light of the party seemed further and further away while the music grew fainter, more distant. Then the right words came to me, of course. *"Rosmorta, help me."*

My parents vanished. One moment they were there, the next they were gone. I walked slowly down the corridor, not wanting to tempt fate more. I moved past those tall arched windows, an uncountable number, with darkness outside and my feet suddenly feeling heavy, so heavy, and my progress was as slow as if it were shifting shingle underfoot instead of cold flagstones. But gradually I moved forwards, dragging my leaden legs, willing my way towards the light. I wondered if those in the room might hear me or see me, and if they would come out to me to help me and welcome me into their company, but they appeared not to notice.

At last it felt I was gaining ground, the open door was closer and the music louder. It called to me and I so wanted to dance if only I could. I stood on the threshold of the doorway and looked in. Still no one noticed me, at first. They carried on dancing and dancing, paying me no attention in the slightest. But then they did, all at once. The music stopped and the dancers turned towards me, and they were all dead. Skulls, grinning, not smiling, in fancy clothes on bony frames.

I woke up, my heart pounding.

The big night at the Golden Lion was a huge success. All the advance tickets sold and people queued up outside to get on-the-night entry. Most of the regular performers from the open mic nights had been given time on the tiny stage to tell jokes, sing or play, but they weren't the only ones. The headliner was someone who was apparently famous on the comedy club circuit for their hard-hitting satire. I'd never heard of her, but that wasn't really surprising as I'm more into book clubs than comedy clubs. But she wasn't the finale. That was going to be Asher himself with the set from his mixtape playing to the audience he'd dreamt of. The pub was crowded. It was good to see how popular Asher had been and how much the community had rallied around this cause.

We had our usual table near the front of the stage. People kept coming up to us and telling us how sorry they were to hear what happened, offering sympathy and saying what a tragedy it was, how Asher was really good and would have made it. None of their words made me feel much better, but the fact that the rest of us were together and this night was taking place was good. I had no idea what would happen next, but there and then we were strong. Jo went to the microphone to introduce Asher's tape. She went over the story of what happened for any who didn't know. Everyone not on the stage was silent for the first time that evening. No one shouted bar orders or chatted among themselves. They were rapt in attention. None of the other entertainers had been granted that. Then they played Asher's words.

It was kind of strange. It was a comedy set, of course, but people didn't at first know whether it was polite to laugh. However, it was so good that they couldn't help smiling, and smiles grew to wide grins and the magic of Asher's best-ever set caught hold. Someone laughed out loud and then everyone was laughing together at the punch lines, which really were inspired. But at last it was over and Asher's voice said his final thank-you and goodbye to an audience from before and to us there that night in his wake.

People cheered and clapped and put more money into the collection boxes. They bought more drinks and said that this wouldn't be the last charity night, and so Asher passed from being some bloke people knew from the pub into local legend. And his spirit lived on in some way at least, and that was perfect.

We left the pub drunk, happiness at the success still mixed with sadness, but in that bitter-sweet way that happens after a while, after a loss, good and bad at the same time. It's probably the best you can hope for. Better than the memory fading, at least.

That mood changed suddenly as someone shouted, "Fire!"

We all looked towards the cliffs. Something was burning. Orange flames from the clifftop were visible in the night sky. It was coming from the direction of Beach View caravan park.

Chapter 17

Caravan of Love

The horrific story of what happened later that night was splashed across the front page of the local newspaper the next day. I can imagine the editor didn't get much sleep while they raced to get the piece written and switched with whatever other news had been deemed most worthy before the death.

Woman Dead in Caravan Park Blaze
A woman died in a fire at a Kent caravan site yesterday.
Firefighters attended the blaze at Beach View caravan park at 11.25pm last night after a 999 call was received by emergency services. An ambulance and fire crews rushed to the cliff-top site, where residents and members of the public were attempting to stop the flames spreading.

The woman was found in a mobile home where the fire is thought to have started. Firefighters used high pressure hoses on the blaze and removed the woman. She was treated by a team from Kent Ambulance Service, but was pronounced dead at the scene. No one else was seriously hurt. Three people were treated for minor burns. There were reports of an explosion before the fire, which quickly took hold, destroying the mobile home.

One witness said: "It happened so fast. There was this loud bang – a real explosion – and I looked over and saw flames. They were huge. There was black smoke too. Loads of us saw it. There was nothing we could do about the caravan. The fire was too fierce. People tried, but they couldn't get close because of the heat."

Sparks from the initial fire spread to neighbouring caravans and caught hold in dry grass at the site, according to the witness.

They added: "Someone shouted to stop it spreading. We could see sparks so we grabbed what we could and started beating them out. Sparks were flying everywhere. They hit the grass and that caught and two other caravans. I've never seen anything like it. It was terrible. Then the fire engine turned up."

Firefighters extinguished the flames at the two neighbouring caravans, which were only slightly damaged, but battled to stop the grass fire reaching nearby woods. They left the scene at 3.45am. Part of the site is still cordoned off.

A spokesman for Kent Police said the cause of the fire and the cause of the woman's death are currently unknown and further investigations will be carried out in the coming days.

I still have that cutting. I felt I had to keep it. What happened was kind of like that, but news stories rarely tell the whole truth. I say that as someone who has now worked on a paper for many years.

When we left the Golden Lion and saw the fire, we knew it was serious. Everyone was pointing up at the cliff and people were saying we should do something. We were shocked. There were people we knew there. And, of course, Charlie was anxious about her own cottage. I know I was too drunk to drive legally but we all piled into Emily and just went up the hill. I think the shock must have sobered me up to some extent and I managed not to crash. Other people were doing the same. Some of those who had been at the charity night were staying at Beach View. They must have been terrified. Many of them would have had kids there, probably just entrusted to some babysitter.

We got to the site before the fire engine showed. I felt relief that was where the fire was rather than Charlie's home, but I guess it wasn't great of me because no one would have died if an empty cottage had burnt down. The fire was fierce – but it was mostly just one mobile home that was burning: Mrs Sweet's. The flames were all over it. No one could have been alive in there. A couple of nearby caravans were starting to smoulder. People were running about. Someone had a fire extinguisher. A few were getting buckets of water. Others were beating patches of burning grass with brooms and shovels and wet towels. But no one could get near Mrs Sweet's home, it was an inferno. Baz and I knew where more firefighting stuff was kept. More extinguishers, sand buckets and beaters – long poles with rubber flaps at the end designed for use at ground-level. All these things were really intended to stop sparks from barbecues getting out of control, not serious conflagrations. We handed the stuff out and tried to organise people.

Then the fire engine arrived and an ambulance. A bunch of burly men in uniforms told us to get out of the way and stand clear, though we held on tight to our beaters and buckets and were ready to step into action again if we needed to. I wondered where Mr and Mrs Sweet could be in all this and I was keeping an eye out, kind of hoping I would see them and know they were safe, but also hoping they wouldn't spot me. There was no sign of her – and no sign of him until the police arrived. He was with them.

That was when all of us except Baz decided to slope off. He felt he should stay. He said he'd be needed, but the rest of our group had no desire to hang around in any of that company and me maybe get done for drink driving. We took the path through the wood to Charlie's place where we opened more cans of booze and hid away anything more incriminating just in case the police called with the breathalyser or worse accusations.

I wasn't in a mood for more alcohol really and I asked Charlie for tea. She made a brew of lemon balm and valerian rather than English Breakfast, stirring in honey at the end. She made us all drink some. It was sickly sweet, but somehow tasted of earth too. I nearly gagged, but Charlie said it was good for shock. I guess that was the state I was still in. My thoughts were reeling at what had happened and I felt cold and shaky. I couldn't be sure that Mrs Sweet was dead, but I suspected it. That was her caravan and she'd loved it. There was surely no other reason she wouldn't have been around to save it from burning. We all speculated on what might have caused the fire and the explosion people said they heard. Maybe a leaky gas cannister and a cigarette? Charlie said hairspray cans can explode if they get too hot. But I knew in my heart of hearts who was really to blame. Me. In my mind I saw that perfect, cheerful caravan, with its bright coloured curtains at the windows and flowers in a little garden inside a miniature picket fence, transformed into a twisted and blackened skeleton as an inferno raged within, and within the flames it seemed I could see a plastic doll shrinking and shrivelling and writhing as it melted, like in the flames at the beach. I wondered if the others thought the same, but I didn't ask and they didn't suggest it.

We waited up long into the night to see if Baz would knock on the door, or the police, but no one did. Eventually Charlie said we should try to sleep. She had blankets and we made space on the floor. I slept only fitfully and had bad dreams that reflected and amplified all my fears.

In the morning Charlie said she'd walk along to the caravan site and find out the news, but the news she brought back was about as bad as it could be. She told us Mrs Sweet was dead and the police had taken Baz to the station for questioning. I was even more shocked, and guilty, and unsure about what to say or do.

The story that was going round the camp was that Suzie had said she had a migraine and had gone to lie down in the caravan earlier in the evening, asking Mr Sweet to take over running the bar. It was unusual, but not unheard of. That was the last time anyone saw her alive, walking across the grass in the moonlight to her home. The bar wasn't very busy that night. The season was winding down and many of the late holidaymakers had been at our charity event at the Lion. When people heard the explosion and spotted the fire, Mr Sweet had rushed outside along with pretty much everyone else there. They'd all run over to the caravan, but the flames were already too fierce for anyone to get close let alone get inside. He'd gone to the office, but said he'd found the phone line dead so he'd jumped in his car and driven down the hill to the first phone box on the way. He was distraught, devastated, angry. It was Mr Sweet who'd blamed Baz. Something about not having fixed some electrics he was supposed to look at, or maybe worse. He'd shouted the accusations angrily and people had to hold him back from attacking our friend. The police had intervened. One officer calmed Mr Sweet down as best they could while others asked Baz to get in their car and come to the station. Maybe he felt that was a safer option than facing Mr Sweet, but he'd gone without arguments.

None of us knew what to do. What do you do when your friend has been accused of something unfairly? Something really serious, like this. I mean, we all assumed it was unfair, but none of us knew. None of us trusted the police. If Baz was charged with something – manslaughter, murder, arson, whatever – what could we do? Life isn't some quaint mystery to be solved by a kindly Miss Marple. Innocent people get nicked all the time. We didn't even dare to ask Rosmorta. We were all still scared in case the police came round to search the cottage and definitely didn't want to be done for graverobbing. We discussed what to do with the skull and other things. Zoe was all for going into the woods and burying the bones and anything else we shouldn't have. Charlie thought we were more likely to get caught doing that than doing nothing. Jo agreed, but said perhaps we should split up; leave Charlie in her place as she was unlikely to be a great suspect while the rest of us went back to Mill Lane and tried to be normal. I admit I was very apprehensive. Not only did I feel guilty, I wondered if someone would mention they had seen me at the site and Mr Sweet might hold as much of a grudge against me as his wife had. In the circumstances, possibly more. Whichever way I looked at it, I felt sooner or later I would be forced to face the music.

The police did come round to ask questions. We answered as truthfully as possible without admitting any wrongdoing. Of course we'd all been together that day, even Baz, well, all afternoon at least. No, none of us had seen him in the morning. No, we wouldn't have done normally. We live in different flats and we didn't get up that early. But all afternoon and then all evening at the Lion. He wasn't working the day of the charity night, we were sure. They didn't seem to have any special questions for me, I was glad to say. They went away and left us alone again.

I needed to think after that, and I needed to be out of the house, so I went for a walk down to the harbour and then along the beach. Not in the direction of the secret bay. Not there. The other way, just to be alone with the wind and the waves and the sand and gravel and little pebbles underfoot, hoping they could somehow blow or wash or crunch away at the spiralling thoughts in my head. They did, sort of. Because really, burning a doll and praying to a skull; these things couldn't actually hurt anyone, could they? It was all coincidence. We'd got carried away, imagining something more like some Gothic tale than real life. Things like that just don't happen in real life, do they? Death was real, life was real. And so long as Baz was released, wasn't held responsible – or me – I didn't care that much that Suzie was dead and gone for good. I'm not proud of thinking that way, but that was the truth of it. That was real. I wasn't going to lie to myself any longer.

I sat down on the shingle and watched a seabird peck the entrails out of some unfortunate fish. That was real too. Sometimes shit just happens, and it's good or bad depending on whether you're the fish or the feaster. It didn't mean anything either. It wasn't some poetic raven or accusing albatross, and this seaside town on the edge of autumn wasn't wheeling with Daphne du Maurier's murderous gulls. It was just life not some stupid novel. I think I felt more miserable at that thought than at anything else that had happened that summer.

Chapter 18

Behind the Wheel

At the heart of *The Name of the Rose* is a vast library, labyrinthine and full of traps for the unwary. It contains much of the knowledge of the known world, yet it is also deadly. I wouldn't have been allowed there, being a woman. I would have been burnt as a witch like the girl from the village, the only female character in Umberto Eco's postmodern novel set in a medieval monastery. At the end of the tale the books burn too, most of them. What is it with fire?

The Name of the Rose is a murder mystery story, but it's really about the meaning of truth in its many forms. Sometimes fiction – although wholly untrue because it is made up in the mind of the author – allows us to explore the convoluted pathways of belief in the search for truth in a way that seems safe. There are no real traps to ensnare us in the passages of the imagination. That's why I love literature and why my own crisis of faith in it didn't last long. Fiction can inspire us, teach us and guide us, although we should always be aware that the real world holds real dangers while those of fiction are only in the mind. But after the fire, things had to be done in the physical world and fiction put aside for the moment. I went to our local library again for information. I took out a book on personal rights and a copy of *Essential Law for Journalists* too. I was going to read these and tackle any modern-day Bernardo Gui with knowledge. I went back to Mill Lane, but there'd been no sign of Baz. Then I told Jo and Zoe I was going to drive round to the police station to see if I could find out what had happened to him. They weren't sure it was a good idea, but I felt I had to go. I owed him that.

The police station was an old Victorian building in red brick not that unlike the library but without the sweet smell of old books. It had one of those Dixon of Dock Green blue lamps over the main door, which you reached up a flight of stone steps probably designed to impress and intimidate in equal measure. I'll admit it took courage to walk up them and go inside, but I took a deep breath and, in my mind, said the words that had been such a charm in my dream. *"Rosmorta, help me."*

Maybe it worked. The officer behind the desk was the same one who had informed us of Asher's death and she recognised me. I asked her if Baz was still there and she told me he was being interviewed. No, she said, I couldn't see him, but I think she took pity on me because she reassured me he was just being questioned as a witness, he hadn't been arrested as far as she knew and she thought they'd probably be finished with him soon. I asked if I could wait. She looked at me thoughtfully for a moment, then said yes, nodding at a row of hard chairs screwed to the floor in a waiting area at one side of the station lobby.

I sat down, got out my library books and started reading as I waited. I learnt that if Baz was only being interviewed as a witness, he'd have been free to leave at any time. I wondered why he hadn't. I also learnt that even if someone is arrested they can normally be held only for 24 hours unless they're actually charged with a crime – although in cases of murder that can be extended. It was really unusual for witnesses to be held at a police station this long, but I was getting used to unusual. Luckily, it wasn't for that much longer.

Baz looked rough when he emerged from the door leading from the bowels of the station. He seemed relieved to see me though. After the thanks for coming, he said he needed cigarettes, then food. I made sure he got both. Sitting down at the closest greasy spoon café we could find, over mugs of strong tea and all-day full English, I asked him what had happened.

"It's kind of a blur," he said, staring at me straight, in between puffs of his third chain-smoked cigarette, his breakfast only half eaten. "I mean, it was a shock, right. Nothing any of us could have thought of, but yeah, I sort of blame myself. I mean, Mr Sweet asked me to look at the lights on the caravan the day before. I had a look, changed a fuse and a bulb. Maybe I should have looked further, but I was busy seeing as I had the next day off for Asher's night. But yes, I kept thinking I'd done something wrong, all the time we were fighting the fire. Then Mr Sweet accused me outright. I mean he did more than that, he was going for me. I went with the police to get away from him as much as anything. I wasn't thinking straight. I mean, we'd all had a lot to drink and the shock and everything.

"I got in the police car and they drove me to the station. They were saying things, but it all sort of washed over me. I wasn't sure if I was being arrested, but someone said no, they just wanted to chat. Could I tell them what happened? I said no, I got there later, I just helped try to put out the fire, but I was kind of zoning out. I mean, Suzie – I know you had reason to hate her, Alice. I get that. She was wrong with what she did to you, but she really wasn't only like you saw her. She put on a face for the public, but I liked her and now she's dead...just so soon after Asher...

"But anyway, at the station someone offered me a cup of tea. They were pretty nice to start with at least. Then my head started swimming and I was sick. I mean really sick. Everything was spinning. I felt dreadful. I think suddenly the shock and drink and everything caught up with me. And someone said I should lie down, have a sleep, and I said yes. They'd leave the questions until later. I just felt so bad. I slept in this cell..."

"They should have called a doctor, if you were sick," I butted in. I'd read that in the book on rights as I was waiting.

"Yeah, well, maybe. I was drunk. I guess they know a drunk when they see one. And judging from the smell I wasn't the first drunk who'd ever pissed and puked in that place. It smelled of bleach but old and stale underneath it all. There was a sort of bed, like a bench fixed to the wall with a blanket and a pillow, but it was hard to sleep on. I lay there kind of thinking, in between everything swimming and feeling sick. I could hear the sounds of the station around me. I'm not sure how real it all was. I think I must have slept and dreamt, but I lost the boundaries. Like the cell I was in seemed so old, I mean older than it did earlier, and the ceiling high and the walls damp and slimy – and there was clanking and chains and moans and screams coming from somewhere beyond the shadows. Look I don't think this was real, I mean I know I must have been dreaming, but it seemed it was. If you were there you'd have thought of some book or story it all came from. Poe or Clive Barker or something. I'm not a complete idiot when it comes to books. I've read a few. Anyway, it was fucking horrible. But I'm glad you're here now, Alice. Thanks for coming for me, and the ciggies and food. I really needed them. They didn't let me smoke. Well, I'd run out you see. But I'm getting ahead of myself.

"Someone came to wake me up the next morning. I guess I did sleep. They said they wanted to ask me questions again. It was someone different from the night before. The shift had changed. Anyway, I got taken to this interview room and I recognised one of the coppers – someone friendly with Mr Sweet. I've seen him at the caravan site a few times. Free drinks at the bar, like I wouldn't be surprised if they're in the same club or something. You'd probably recognise him too if you saw him.

"Anyway, this copper and another ask me questions. I'm still feeling groggy. They give me a cup of water, but nothing else. One of them's smoking. I ask if I can have a cigarette, but they say no, later, after I've answered some questions. I ask if I'm arrested, and they say no, not yet, but I'd better be co-operative. And I don't really know what to do. Someone like me – it doesn't pay not to be co-operative.

"So, I answer their questions. I go over it again and again. Yes, I mention about changing the fuse too, but no I didn't spot anything else wrong and no I wasn't there at all the day of the fire. In the evening I was at the Lion. I was really losing the plot, honestly. Then, suddenly, someone comes in and they have a mutter then they say they've asked enough questions for now at least. So I ask if I can go and the one I recognise, he smiles like this real crocodile smile and says of course I can, I could have gone any time I liked. The bastard."

Baz finished his breakfast and I drove him back to Mill Lane so he could get some proper sleep. I told the others what had happened, but none of us really knew what to do except hope for the best. And I carried on reading my books and learning about the law. It would be pretty useful if I did get that job on the paper, but probably not that much help for Baz or the rest of us if the police decided to give us more of a hard time. At least I'd be safe from being burnt as a witch – unlike the girl in the village – despite the lingering guilt I still felt of maybe causing Suzie Sweet's death.

Then the next day came around and we hadn't heard anything more from the police, so we decided to go back up to see Charlie to find out if she knew anything. I drove slowly past Beach View so we could peer into the site. It was deserted. The blackened shell of Suzie's home was still there. It looked like there was police tape around it. There was more across the gate and a sign saying the caravan park was closed. It looked deserted too. I should have expected it, really.

Charlie told us that the site had been evacuated. There had been police and fire investigators busy there all of the day before. They'd asked people questions, but any remaining holidaymakers had been relocated to another caravan park further along the coast after they'd given statements about what they'd seen. Mr Sweet's car had been parked outside the main building until evening at least, but today there was no sign of him and Charlie had no idea where he was. Now the investigators had gone too and Beach View was locked up and devoid of life.

We all wanted to go and have a look at the site now it was safe to do so. We took the footpath. Even that had a bit of police tape stretched between two trees at the edge of the wood, but it wasn't exactly hard to walk around it. It was so quiet and still, eerily familiar yet strange without the sights and sounds of holidaymakers – no children playing, people drinking or eating, friendly chat or laughter, just the sound of the wind and the gulls and the sea in the distance. The smell of smoke and cinders lingered. It was like a ghost town full only of the shadows of memories from summer days that had passed. We wandered across the lonely fields, spotting brown oblongs in green grass marking where the private caravans had so recently stood, then walking between the static mobile homes, locked and forsaken, their windows dark or curtains closed. We stood in front of the burnt wreckage, outside the circle of tape, not knowing quite what to do or say. No one wanted to breach that line.

My own thoughts were in turmoil. Of course I'd been angry with Mrs Sweet, but I would never have wished this fate on her. Not really. That wasn't what I meant when I burnt the doll. It had all been a game in my head, hadn't it? But I said I'd be honest with myself; truthful, didn't I. No, it hadn't been a game. I had wished her ill, but I'd never wished her dead. In my mind I pleaded silently, *"Rosmorta, did you think I wanted to kill her? Please Rosmorta, please tell me what I can do to make up for this. Please don't let Baz get accused. Or anyone else. Please?"*

Maybe my prayer was answered. No one did get charged over the fire or the death of Suzie Sweet. It was another accident, apparently. A leaky gas cannister and a cigarette left burning, just like Charlie had said. Apparently Suzie'd taken some migraine medicine that had knocked her out. She wouldn't have seen the fire start. And it would have been quick, the death, or so they said. So life went on again for us, sort of normal, but not really. Everything seemed that bit darker and emptier as the autumn nights really set in.

Chapter 19

True Faith

There's a cliché that what you don't see can be scarier than what you do. It's a cheap trick in old movies, from when special effects couldn't deliver believable monstrosities, but it's also used in books. Lovecraft was famous for his indescribable horrors. In *At the Mountains of Madness*, when his protagonists are escaping from a vast, ancient, sentient ooze of slime and eyeballs, he wrote that the written word "...can never even suggest the awfulness of the sight itself". It lets the reader's imagination do the extra work, to envision their own worst nightmare, something they personally find terrifying. Regardless of the cliche there's some truth in the idea. Despite all I wrote earlier about the imagination being safer than reality, in this way imagination has a knack of proving that wrong, of going further than either written words or real life. I have to admit I didn't see exactly what happened at one pivotal incident after Suzie's death. That was at a séance to contact her ghost.

The reason I wasn't there in the room when it happened is that I'd been told I wasn't trusted, I wasn't wanted. I had been cast from the inner circle of friendship and could only linger on the edges, having fallen from grace. Knowing that, feeling the ache of no longer belonging, felt worse than the scariest ghost story I could imagine or the terror that gripped me in the woods when I should have been alone that night. So, I can tell you what happened to me and what I saw and experienced and did, and I can tell you the stories I only heard afterwards, about what happened inside when the others tried to contact the dead.

It was Baz who suggested another séance. Not to try to bring Asher's spirit to our table, that never felt quite right. No, it was Suzie Sweet's ghost who Baz wanted to summon. He never believed the official statement that the fire was just an accident. I'm sure he still felt guilty, sure he'd missed something when he fixed the fuse. Or maybe it was just the way that Mr Sweet returned to Beach View not long after the fire and, as soon as he was allowed, started getting the place done up, the wreckage of the old mobile home swept away and a new one in its place. He'd asked Baz to come back to work there, and Baz had said yes. It wasn't like he had any other job to go to. But he'd thought long and hard about it before he went back to help with the task of making the site inviting for next year's guests. But he said he had bad dreams at night, as did I.

"I don't like it," I admitted, as we all sat around Charlie's table again one grey and grim afternoon, after Baz had suggested the séance. "Suzie always hated me. She'll point her ghostly finger at me, even if her death was an accident, why would she stop hating me after she's dead?"

"I don't believe it was you. I think there's more to it and I want to find out the truth." Baz had said that before, but however often he said it I still felt guilty and I'm sure the others remembered me burning the doll, and the words I'd said. Would I have done it if I'd known what would happen? That's what I lay awake wondering when I wasn't dreaming of fire. And yes, I guess knowing the truth would help, or could help, or not. I just didn't know. I'd said I wanted the truth, but I wasn't sure this was the way to get it.

"The truth is important..." said Jo, slowly and thoughtfully, "but how can we know that the spirit board won't lie? Surely there's a better way of finding out what happened?"

"We can't ask the people who were staying at the caravan site, they've all moved on. And presumably the police have done that already," I pointed out. "Is there likely to be any evidence the police or fire investigators didn't go over?"

"There might be," said Charlie. "If there was something the police didn't find, a séance could give us a clue about something to look for. Suzie put on a face for the public, but she would have had a private side too and secrets. Baz knows that... And maybe something happened that afternoon when Baz wasn't there."

Zoe nodded. "I think we should go for it, do the séance. We might not learn anything, but then again, we might. We won't know unless we try. And I was there too when the doll burnt. I could have stopped you, Alice, we all could. Any of us, but we didn't. If Suzie's dead because of it then we need to know. Not that we could go to the police, if that's the truth, even if we wanted to, but we need to do this. Just for us. For you and for Baz and for all of us. So we know."

Was I on trial here, I wondered, trial by séance? If I was, what could I do or say? I wanted to find out the truth, didn't I? But I wasn't happy. Jo was still at least partly with me in reticence. She frowned. "I still don't think it's a good idea. Even if we contact Suzie, she might not know what happened. Surely ghosts aren't omniscient? They might be vindictive and lie, just like living people. I think we shouldn't stir up stuff that doesn't need stirring. Learn from our mistakes, but move on and forwards, put the past behind us. Let the dead rest."

"Perhaps we've stirred up the past too much already to stop now. And perhaps doing this will help lay the dead to rest," Charlie suggested.

"I want to do this, but only if Alice's okay with it too," said Baz.

"I'll go along with it if you all need me to." I wasn't sure I could say anything else, in the circumstances.

Charlie said: "I think we should vote. We all need to be in favour. If anyone isn't then we leave it be. Raise your hand if you want to do the séance, if you want to see if we can talk to

Suzie's spirit and see if we can learn what her spirit can spell out."

No one raised a hand quickly, but Zoe was the first to do so, then Baz almost immediately after. I raised mine next – because I'd look as guilty as I felt if I didn't. Then Jo looked at Zoe, raised her hand, probably just to show support rather than because she really wanted to. Charlie raised her hand last and nodded.

"Okay, its agreed. Let's do it."

We couldn't do it immediately, though, Charlie said. We had to wait. We needed something that belonged to Suzie, something she used or wore often, or even better a lock of her hair. Baz said he'd see what he could do. He'd look around the caravan park, there must be something belonging to her still there.

What he brought to the cliff-edge cottage a few days later was a make-up bag in shiny plastic with fake gold trim, some rip-off of a designer label I suspected. It was so Suzie it made me shiver. Baz said he'd found it behind the bar, presumably just where she'd left it before going back to her caravan for her last sleep. Inside was a comb with a few strands of her black hair between its teeth, a small mirror, lipstick, a nail file and a bottle of bright red polish. There was something awful in seeing them, but none of us could resist inspecting the relics. We handed round the comb with a mixture of disgust and morbid fascination. I picked up the tiny mirror and looked into it, seeing my own reflection and realising that the last person to do that would never do so again. Zoe took the cap off the lipstick and extended its glossy scarlet core. The tip was an oval, slightly worn with the impression of Suzie's once-living lips. She tested the colour in a livid streak across the back of her hand. At that, Charlie stopped with a look of shock, then dropped the comb that had been in her own hands and grabbed Zoe's wrist.

"Don't do that! We shouldn't really be touching any of it. We should put it all back in the bag. We need to keep the link to Suzie as pure as possible."

Zoe nodded, hurriedly resealed the lipstick and returned it to the plastic holder, snapping shut the mock-gold clip on the bag, then wiped her hand, smearing the waxy residue into an indistinguishable blur, but unable to get rid of it completely. *Yeah, but I'm more like Lady Macbeth*, I thought. She put the bag in the middle of the table, where it held our gaze in uncertain silence for a while; a silence broken by Baz.

"So, when are we going to do it?"

"Séances are best done by moonlight," said Charlie. "We should wait until night, and gather everything else we need, including a new glass."

I think we all remembered how the last one had shattered when we first named Rosmorta, but we had others like it at Mill Lane. I drove back to get one of them while the others remained at Charlie's cottage to set things up. That was when the tide turned further against me, as the others planned and schemed when I wasn't there.

There had been a set of six wineglasses at one time, which got shared between the two flats. They were oddly short and stubby, the bowls not as large as modern ones tend to be, while the glass was thick and a bit uneven. I'd often wondered how old they were, when we'd used them, because they looked kind of antique. But there were only four now. One had smashed in our first séance and the next had been thrown by Baz in his fit of anger. Both must have taken some force, I thought, as I looked at the thickness of those remaining. I wondered if another would shatter that night and, if so, then there'd be just three. I studied the four vessels, wondering if there was one that would be better to take than any other, or any with slight chips that meant they should be disregarded, but in the end I just took one at random. I looked around the flat to see if there was something else that might be needed, but couldn't think of anything, so I put the unlucky chalice into my bag and drove back up the hill.

Charlie let me into the cottage and I could see they had already set up the table. There was the board with its stuck-on Scrabble tiles and the plastic-and-fake-gold make-up bag at the edge, before Rosmorta's skull in her place of honour at the head. Chairs had been placed evenly around the table too, four of them, with Zoe, Jo and Baz occupying three. They seemed very quiet and were looking at me. There was a tension in the atmosphere that made me feel uncomfortable, although I put that down to concerns at what we were about to do. The rest of the seats were pushed back against the wall. I took the glass out of my bag and put it on the table, then wondered whether I should sit at the fourth chair or pull up a fifth, when Charlie delivered the verdict.

"Alice, we've been talking, thinking about this séance. We think you should sit it out. I'm sorry, but you were right when you pointed out that Suzie's spirit might be more co-operative if you aren't here."

I looked around at the faces of my friends, not knowing what to say, feeling betrayed.

"I'm really sorry. If it was up to me..." Baz's voice trailed off and he looked away.

"We're all really sorry," said Jo. "Please don't be upset..."

"Yes, really sorry," echoed Zoe. "You don't have to go far..."

"You can wait outside, if you like," said Charlie. "We'll tell you what happens and you can come in afterwards. Honestly, it's for the best. The sun's nearly setting, so we'll start soon. Why not pour a cup of tea – it's a chai blend. Take it out to the garden? Sit on a bench and wait?"

So that was what I did. I sat on a twisty driftwood bench with a view over the garden to the cliff edge and the sea, nursing the tin mug of spiced tea along with my bruised feelings. If I'd known I'd be sitting and waiting I'd have brought a book to read, probably, although the light was going. But I hadn't so I just sat and watched and listened to the sounds of the wind and waves.

It had been a grey day with hints of rain along with gusts of wind, yet there had been a few breaks in the clouds. Sometimes the wind had dropped and one such moment happened as the moon rose over the water. The low, silvery light reflected across the sea as it had that night when I first saw my attic room at Mill Lane. It made the drops of water on the plants and leaves and everything in the garden sparkle. Even the spiderwebs glistened with moon-struck moisture, connecting stalks and branches and gaps in the hedgerow. It was beautiful, perfect; a moment I wouldn't have seen if I'd been inside with the others. That brief perspective gave me hope and reminded me that however dark things seemed now, it would, perhaps, soon be over. Maybe I'd be vindicated, I mused as I sipped my chai. The door to the cottage would open and I'd be welcomed back into the light and the company of my friends, and I'd know the truth, and the truth would be good. Maybe.

But that moment of peace and beauty wasn't to last. Dark clouds rolled across the sky obscuring the moon and the wind rose. Then came the rain. What would the history of horror stories be without dark and stormy nights? It was a cliché worse than indescribable terrors long before Edward Bulwer-Lytton wrote about the violent gusts of wind that rattled London rooftops in 1830. There were many in 1987. Everyone who's old enough remembers October 16th, but there were storms before that and this was one such night when a tempest grew and raged enough to wake the dead, which was, of course, exactly what my friends were trying to do.

Chapter 20

Alone

The rain began as the occasional splatter and I pulled up the hood of my jacket against that and the wind. Turning my back to the inclement weather, I finished my rapidly cooling mug of milky tea blended with spices. At the bottom, all that was left of the sweet drink with its undertones of nutmeg, cinnamon and star anise, was a brown, woody sludge. I put the mug down next to me on the bench and looked out across the garden again, but the sky was heavy with storm clouds in the night and I could barely see anything in the darkness. I looked around. A single candle flame flickered in the cabin window, placed there to guide the spirits from their otherworldly realm into the light of the séance. It seemed hugely welcoming to me, out in the gloom and cold and wet of the rainy night-time garden, but I wasn't the one being invited.

The rain and wind intensified. I realised I had to take better cover. I longed so much to knock on the door and ask to be let back inside, but knew I mustn't do that. I thought of taking refuge in Emily, but my car was parked at the barrier in the road. It not only seemed a long walk in the dark and the rain, but would also mean I wasn't within sight of the cottage. The others wouldn't know where I was and I wouldn't see when they'd finished their chat with the dead and opened the door to invite me back in. At least, I hoped they'd open the door and invite me back as soon as they'd finished, but I was suddenly struck by the fear that they would have forgotten I was waiting. It was an unpleasant thought.

The only thing to do was to take shelter under the trees at the edge of the wood which curled around the lower side of the cottage, bordering the garden on the other side from the cliff-edge. From there I could watch the cottage, even if I could no longer see the front door or the candle in the window. Although visibility was low, when the séance ended presumably they would light lamps and I would see a brighter glow spread out across the plant beds, even if my friends didn't immediately open the door to welcome me back. I'd take any sign as my cue to re-enter anyway. So, I left the tin mug to fill with rain on the wooden seat and picked my way across the sodden garden in the dark to a gap in a hedge at its edge. I passed through that, brushing away strands of sticky spiderweb as I entered the wood.

Leaning back against the trunk of a tree, I let its canopy protect me a little from the rain. The odd drop fell through the thinning autumn leaves on branches that were creaking and swaying in the now gale-force winds, but mostly I was sheltered. I waited there for a while, I'm not sure how long. It was hard to judge time – whether just a minute or two had passed, or many. I stared through the gaps in the hedge across dark space at the silhouette of the cottage.

After a while – as I said, I don't really know how long – I thought it seemed that I spotted something moving around in the garden, sniffing around the bench where I'd just been sitting. It was a glimpse only, seen through the corner of my eye at the edge of my vision. I wasn't quite certain what it was, a shadowy shape, barely distinguishable from all the other shadows, just darker than the rest of the darkness, if that was possible. I was unsure if it was just the wind blowing at a bush of roses or if it was some animal desperate for shelter like myself – a melanistic fox or a stray dog with shaggy black fur, perhaps. It could have been just my imagination. I watched intensely, trying to work out if something was really there or not. I came to the conclusion that, if it was real, it didn't seem quite like any natural creature I could think of. I got the impression of something moving strangely. I couldn't quite make out how many legs it had, whether four legs or hunched over but on two, or maybe more... Suddenly, for a moment, the wind dropped and I felt that whatever it was, if it was anything, had noticed me, perhaps sniffed my scent, sensed me in some other way. It seemed to stop still and, maybe, look towards me. Of course, again, that could have been because the wind was no longer shaking the leaves and stalks, but maybe it wasn't.

Just in case, I slunk behind the wide trunk of the tree where I was sheltering, but then I had to peek out from my hiding place just to know whether the thing, if it was a thing, was still looking at me. Or worse, was silently picking its way across the dark, wet garden towards me and that my concealment was futile. I looked, but really couldn't be certain. It's easy to scare oneself with imaginings on nights when one's alone. But what if my friends in their séance had attracted something? What if this was something they hadn't meant to summon, and which couldn't get into their protected circle of joined hands around the table, but was outside, hungry and even more lonely than me? The wind had risen again and was howling around the headland. The rain was torrential and the darkness almost complete.

For me, the most scary chapter of the *Lord of the Rings* is when the Hobbits hide from an unseen rider they hear coming along the road behind them. They're unsure who it is at first, but it becomes clear it's a Nazgul, a Ringwraith, a spectral hunter who can sniff its prey by supernatural means. Despite being well hidden in a hollow behind a tree, Frodo is filled with a sudden unreasoning fear of discovery. That was how I felt, hiding in the woods myself that night. I had no magic ring, but I found myself thinking what I'd done that might attract the attention of some hungry spirit. I felt I had to move, to get away, to escape whatever awful fate might await me if I was discovered by whatever I felt uncomfortably certain had sniffed my trail.

I crept deeper into the woods. It was pitch black, or so it seemed at first. I moved cautiously, slowly, feeling the ground ahead with the tips of my toes before putting pressure on my feet, my arms and hands outstretched to feel whatever branches or thorns were in my way, always aware that if I veered from a straight course, I could find myself at the edge of the cliff itself; my fingers reaching into thin air too late to save me from a deathly plunge.

I realise how foolish this sounds. I realise that trying to pick my way through a forest in darkness seems crazy now, but at the time I felt it was all I could do. And despite my caution, twigs scratched at my head and face, and brambles tore at my clothes and arms, but still I kept going, deeper into the wood. I was lost, alone, not knowing where I was going or from what, really, I was trying to escape. *"Rosmorta, help me, please!"* I gave the silent, mental plea almost by instinct now.

Then, suddenly, I started to sense a way out. I saw a shimmer of light ahead, faint, distant, wavering and uncertain, but I felt sure I had seen it and could head towards it. I caught glimpses of other tiny lights too, it seemed, at the corners of my vision, just like the moonlight on the spiderwebs I'd seen in the garden earlier. It seemed to me that if I went towards the light, however faint, and trod the path between those uncertain spiderwebs, I would find my way through the dark wood. Or perhaps it was more that I felt I was being led somewhere and I had to go on.

Sometimes, when you're staring into absolute darkness, you start to see things that can't possibly be there. Flashes or glimmers of light like little stars can be caused by a bang on the head scattering the signals your nerves are sending to your brain. Sometimes they're the aura of a migraine, or even, if you're really unlucky, a torn retina. Often they're just the imagination playing tricks. I can't be sure why I saw what I thought I saw, but following lights led me, eventually, out of the wood at the far side to the edge of the caravan park.

The rain pummelled into me again as soon as I left the shelter of the trees, but I felt a huge sense of relief to be in a place where there were real lights. The electric lamps on posts that were dotted around the site intermittently were swaying under the force of the wind. The yellow circles they cast were sweeping around the rows of mobile homes like erratic spotlights without focus. Even the caravans were swaying. It seemed everything was in motion, dancing to the howling tempest's tune; everything except the site's main building with the bar and the office. From these windows ushered a welcoming brightness.

I pushed against the wind and picked my way towards the bar then peered through the plate glass. Under the glowing fluorescent strips, I could see the chairs and tables were neatly arranged, but the place was deserted. No sign of life. I tried the door, but it was locked. Once again, I felt utterly alone. I might not have been exactly popular at Beach View, but if the bar had been open, I could have taken shelter there. No one would have turned me away. I could have bought a drink and sat in the dry, in safety, in human company. But it was not to be.

The other lit window was the one to the office. It was go there, or go back. I made my choice and went to meet the devil I knew. Creeping along the wall to make the most of the shelter, I approached the office window and cautiously looked in. At first, I thought it was deserted too. There was a desk and chair, unoccupied, yet looking as though someone had used them recently. Papers were scattered all over the surface of the desk and the chair was at a slight angle and pushed a little back. On the desk, between an ancient Bakelite phone and a plastic holder for pens, was a glass, a whisky bottle and a tin ashtray full of butts. I glanced quickly around the rest of the room, lined with shelves of box files and huge old gunmetal grey cabinets with paper labels on each drawer. No one was standing at them. The door at the rear, leading further into the block, was closed. Then I looked down at the floor beside the desk and I saw him there, Mr Sweet, lying motionless on the chequered linoleum, his eyes closed. I rushed to the door on my side of the office and tried to open it. I had to see if I could help. The door was locked.

I stood back, fighting the urge to panic. I shouted out for help, but no one came and my words disappeared into the wind. There were no lights at any of the caravan windows. I was alone, I knew that. I looked around for a way of getting into the locked room, but nothing seemed obvious. Then, shoving my hands into my jacket pockets, my fingers touched something. A hard pebble, smoothed by the sea, but possibly capable of breaking glass a second time, and I knew what I had to do. *"Thank you, Rosmorta,"* I think I whispered. I pulled my hand into the sleeve of my jacket to protect the skin and, gripping the stone, smashed hard against the thin pane of the office window.

He wasn't dead. I could see him breathing, but he wasn't conscious. I knew not to move him, in case he had a broken neck or whatever, so I used the phone to call 999. As I was dialling, I saw a sealed envelope addressed to Baz among the papers on the desk. I didn't pick it up immediately, but I kept thinking about it as I was waiting for the ambulance to arrive. It seemed I had to wait for hours, but it was probably less than half an hour. During the time I found some plastic and tape to seal the window, and yes, at the last moment, I did take the envelope. I put it in my pocket, unopened. I was tempted to look inside, I admit, but it felt wrong to interfere that much.

The paramedics asked what had happened. I explained that I didn't really know, and how I had found him. I did it as briefly as possible without going into details about my earlier foolish-sounding fears. They moved him onto a stretcher and carried him into their care, then asked if I wanted to come with him. No, I told them. No need for that.

"Take care then," one said as they were leaving. "Second time we've been up this way tonight. Try not to give us a reason to come up here a third time."

"What happened earlier?" I shouted as they closed the doors, but plainly I wasn't heard and their comment hadn't been intended to scare me. Nevertheless, I was scared. My hands were shaking as I found a spare set of keys in the desk drawer to lock up after myself and leave the office as securely as I could before going back to the cottage and the others, who I hoped were fine and by that time wondering what had happened to me. In the drawer I also found a small working flashlight, which I took to guide me along the way.

For my return to Charlie's place I went as quickly as possible via the road. It might be a longer route, but there was no way I was risking the woods even if I did now have a torch. I ran when I felt it was safe to do so, only slowing when I reached the end of the road. As I got closer, though, I realised something was very wrong. There were no lights on at the cottage, but I could hear the front door banging in the wind. I called out, but no one answered. I rushed up to the cottage door, which was swinging on its hinges. Pointing my light inside, I saw chaos.

Broken tiles, splintered wood and other debris covered the table and spilled over the floor. Rain was pouring in through a huge gaping hole in the ceiling. A massive broken tree branch protruded through it. What was worse, I could see tell-tale splatters of blood among the rubble. So, this was where the ambulance drivers had been earlier and I had no way of knowing what had happened or what to do next.

Shining my light once more over the ruin, I spotted something I couldn't leave behind. The eye socket of a skull stared at me through the wreckage. I knew that if I did nothing else, I had to rescue Rosmorta. It was important that I save her, to hide her and keep her away from any other prying eyes. I gingerly stepped inside the cottage, glancing up at the roof in fear of more tiles and timbers tumbling in and burying me. None fell. I carefully moved away the smaller pieces of debris and, once again, eased the skull out of a precarious grave. She seemed unharmed. I put her inside my jacket and, hugging her close, went back to the car. There, I wrapped her safely in my sleeping bag and drove home to Mill Lane.

Chapter 21

Somewhere Out There

"Where the fuck were you?" demanded Baz when I got back to Mill Lane. He was the only one there. He seemed more angry than worried. And I was suddenly angry too.

"Only fucking taking shelter from the rain. What else did you expect me to do when you left me out in the garden? Oh, and saving a fucking life too!" I shouted.

He glared at me. "Whose life? You weren't there to help Zoe."

"What?" I was suddenly cold with concern, thinking of the collapsed roof, the blood... "What happened?"

Baz told me, at least he told me what happened from his perspective.

Everything I've related up until this point is what I experienced. Admittedly this happened a long while ago, and memory is a fallible thing, especially as one gets older. I've been as truthful as possible and I'll continue to be as truthful as I can. However, what happened inside the cottage, while I was outside and traversing the dark wood and then trying to save a life, I've had to piece together from what others said, and they didn't all say the same things.

If I was writing an article for a newspaper I'd interview those involved, if they'd talk to me. I'd try to speak to witnesses, pick the choicest quotes, ask for a statement from the emergency services and add a bit about the background: the fire and the deaths. If I had room, I'd tie it in to other accounts of damage in the wake of the storm. The supernatural might come into it, if I could find a juicy angle. Depending on the nature of the paper I was writing for, that could be to paint Charlie, Jo, Zoe and Baz as dabbling in dangerous black magic, a depraved drug-fuelled coven of low-life scroungers who looted graves and did other things no respectable person would dream of. Or my paper's readership might be sympathetic with séances, believers in ghosts, and looking for proof of existence beyond the grave. People can find such stories console them as they get closer to their own moment when the truth of life's greatest mystery is revealed. Or I might poke fun at them for believing such ridiculous things. Didn't they realise science had banished all the ghosts to the bad joke box? But I'm not writing this to some editor's orders, and at the time I just wanted to find out what happened. This is what Baz said.

"I was having second thoughts about the séance," he admitted to me, almost immediately. "I know I was the one who suggested it, but I shouldn't have. It was a mistake. I wanted to find out what had happened, really happened. It was creepy up at Beach View, working with Mr Sweet as the boss and Suzie not there, and he didn't want her mentioned. At all. He wanted all trace of her gone. He never blamed me, after that first time when he did and the police questioned me. But after that, no, he just wanted everything cleared up and he was acting like a model boss. But it was fake, or maybe it was his way of dealing with it. It's not like an old bloke's gonna cry, is it? But I couldn't help wondering...

"When Charlie said I had to get something that belonged to her... I knew about the make-up bag. I'd seen it, tucked behind the bar. She always kept it there. She'd take it to the ladies and redo her hair or nails or something. She always wanted to look good. I hadn't told him. He'd have thrown it out. In a way I wanted to have a reason to take it, an excuse. But then, when everyone was opening it, taking stuff out, trying it on... I felt like calling the whole thing off, just take the bag and stuff and keep it to remember her... Look, Alice, I didn't love her, but I cared about her... But then I thought that we'd gone that far and I wanted the truth...

"After you left, I mean the first time, to get the glass, we set things up, got out the skull and the board. We drank some chai and chatted about what we were going to do. It was Zoe who said maybe you shouldn't be there after all. I thought we'd discussed it and agreed it was okay. But Zoe started acting kind of strange, even then. And Charlie said maybe she was right, and Jo always goes along with whatever Zoe wants... I felt bad about it, but it wasn't raining then... Anyway, you leaving, the second time, closing the door behind you, it felt like things changed. I can't describe it. Like we'd made a bad choice. But it was too late..."

No, it wasn't, I thought. *You could have opened the door and invited me back.* But I said nothing to Baz then. No point, not really. What was done was done.

"So, what happened?" I asked, as neutral as possible, and he continued.

"Everyone was keyed-up. Sat around the table. But it was like no one wanted to start. No one wanted to be the first to put their finger on the glass and invite our ghosts. People changed the subject, sort of, I mean Zoe changed the subject. She said she was cold, then Jo fussed over something. Then Charlie changed her mind about what we were going to do. How we were going to do it. She said we'd try the spirit board later, but first we'd just ask Rosmorta. Ask her to guide Suzie's spirit to us and for that we needed darkness apart from a single light. She lit a candle in the front window, but turned off the other lamps. I could hardly see a thing. It was so dark. Charlie told us to hold hands and to keep holding on, no matter what happened. There were just the four of us, of course. I was holding Charlie's hand on one side and Zoe's on the other.

"Charlie spoke; the rest of us stayed quiet. She asked Rosmorta to guide Suzie's ghost to us, so we could talk to her. Then she went silent. No one felt they could say anything. We were just waiting... Nothing happened immediately. I don't know what I expected, but there was just the cold and the dark and holding hands and the sounds of people breathing...inside the cottage, at least. And I wondered if we'd annoyed her, Rosmorta I mean, by shutting you out. It seemed to go on forever and I wanted to say something, but I couldn't. We all sat there, gripping hands in the darkness, listening, breathing. The sounds became louder outside. I could hear the rain and wind. It was in the trees... I could hear the branches creaking and knocking against the back wall and the roof. I'd never really noticed that before. It was so loud. And there was something hitting at the door. It had to be branches, I guess. Then I could hear other noises too, once I'd started really listening, quieter, more like scratching. Like there was something trying to get in. I think the others heard it too, but Charlie said we had to keep holding hands. The rain got louder and louder, rattling against the window. I thought about you, out there. I wondered if it was you at the door... But then I thought it couldn't be. I thought you'd go shelter in your car. That's what I would have done. You'd have been okay there. I told myself.

"My mind wasn't really on the séance, all I could think of was what was outside. I told myself it was just the storm. Nothing would happen, we'd made a mistake. But then something did happen. It got colder. Really cold. Icy. I thought perhaps it was a draught got through a crack or under the door. I know I shivered. Then the candle spluttered and went out and the room got even darker. I felt Zoe's hand clench. She gripped my fingers tight, dug her nails into my palm. They were long and sharp. And, well, well, Zoe doesn't *have* long nails... Then she spoke, only... well, it was odd..."

"But *what* did she say?" I interrupted.

Baz shook his head. He seemed reluctant to say whatever it was he remembered. He looked away from me.

"Was it *me*? Did she blame me?" I asked, worried.

"No, no," said Baz, hurriedly.

"Are you sure?"

"No, no, of course I'm not sure. Not now, but that was how it seemed."

"So, what *did* she say?" I had to know.

"She just asked where she was and who was there, like she was lost and couldn't see or feel. *'Who's there?' 'Where am I?'* Those long nails were digging into my skin. I didn't know why she was asking as she must have felt my hand too, surely? I could feel her arms were shaking too, but she kept asking, *'Who's there?' 'Where am I?'* again and again. Then Charlie spoke. She sounded calm, still, at first. *'We're all friends,'* she said, or something like that. Then Zoe, or Suzie – I mean, it felt like her hand, Alice. She shouted out. It might have been Zoe. *'Let me go!'* That was what she shouted. And she tried to pull her hand away, maybe, or maybe it was like something was pulling her away and she was trying to hold on. I can't be sure. But she did pull away and stood up. It was still so dark. I could vaguely make out shadows. Someone was moving around. I guess Zoe. There was a bang, I think she knocked something over, but the storm was loud outside too, I could hear the wind howling and something, the branches, battering on the roof and scraping. I think maybe Jo got up as well. It was hard to make out where all the sounds were coming from, who was moving around in the dark. Someone shouted, *'Stop it!'* and, *'Sit down!'* No one sat down, though, I don't think. I hadn't got up before, but I did then. Charlie'd let go of my hand by then too. I thought we needed light. So I went over to the window, I felt my way mostly, around the table end. I thought maybe I'd relight the candle. I didn't have any matches...

"I stood there, by the front wall, by the window next to the door, with the unlit candle, not knowing what was happening or what to do, like a big idiot. Then suddenly there was this huge crash and things were falling in all around me, scratching my face and arms and lashing at me, and the rain came flooding in. This branch, this massive branch. It'd burst through the ceiling, bringing down tiles and bits of wood and dust. I was choking..."

"What about the others?" I broke into the flow of what he was saying, but I had to know.

"They were under the branch. They were under it when it fell. Someone was screaming. I just stood there, Alice. I didn't know what to do...what to do... Then something grabbed my leg... It was Charlie. She was okay, scratched, but okay. She crawled out from under the branch.

"When we lit the candle... Zoe wasn't okay. The branch, the roof. She was trapped underneath it. She wasn't conscious... Jo was bleeding too, but not bad. We got Jo out, sat her down on the bench outside. I saw your mug there... Charlie found a waterproof and a torch. She went and called an ambulance. I was so fucking useless! But why weren't you waiting Alice? Why weren't you there, waiting on the bench, or even taking shelter in the car, like I thought you'd be?"

He looked at me like I'd disappointed him, and again I felt like protesting. *It wasn't my fault.* But I didn't.

"I wish I had been. I'm sorry. I'm so sorry. Zoe...what did the ambulance people say? Where is she?"

"She's at the hospital, so's Jo. Charlie dropped me off here, on her bike. She must have gone back to the cottage..."

"No. She's not there. I've been there. I'd have seen her."

"Then where the fuck is she?" Baz shouted it at me. Then he looked away.

"Look, I'm sorry," he said, but he didn't sound it. "I don't know what we should do. I keep wondering what caused it all. Was it us? Did we do something wrong? I keep remembering what Asher said. We should have listened to him, Alice. We really should have."

"Yeah," I said. "Maybe we should."

I left Baz at Mill Lane and drove to the hospital. Maybe I'd find Charlie there, I thought. I didn't, but I did find Zoe. Jo, stitched and bandaged, was at her bedside. Zoe wasn't conscious. Jo turned and looked at me.

"Where the hell have you been all this time?" she asked, and I realised even Jo had turned against me.

Chapter 22

Girlfriend in a Coma

"I'm sorry." I seemed to be saying that a lot that night, but it wasn't the time or place to try to excuse myself, I realised that. "Baz told me Zoe got hit by a falling branch... How is she?"

Jo shook her head. "I don't know, Alice. I don't know. Concussion they say, but they don't yet know if it's worse than that. They don't know if there's brain injury. They don't know when...if...she'll wake..."

"Can I do anything? Can I get anything? Are you okay? I mean apart from..." I wanted to help, but didn't know what or how I could make things better.

"I'm just scratched," said Jo, although she looked worse than that to me. "I'll be okay. And no, there's nothing you can get. Nothing you can do. We trusted you, Alice. I trusted you. But all the time you were just using us."

"What?" The accusation seemed to come out of nowhere and hit me with astonishment. I realised I'd not waited in the car during the séance, but this was more and I didn't understand. "What do you mean?"

"Baz told us. He told us when you were back at Mill Lane, getting that glass. He said you weren't writing about the coast – you were writing about us! Your book was all about us! Like you were spying on us or something! Zoe went crazy when she heard. You were just using us, Alice. You never told us what you were really up to. You should have done. You manoeuvred us and manipulated us and lied to us. Zoe said she didn't want you in the room when we did the séance. Said maybe Suzie was right. How can we know how much of this is your doing? The weird shit, the deaths even... And then this happened... Well, I

141

hope it makes a good book, but I want nothing more to do with you. Just leave us alone." Jo looked away from me.

I'd wanted to shout denial, but in my heart of hearts I realised some of it was true. If she'd burst into tears, I'd have stayed. But she didn't. She looked down at Zoe, lying there unconscious. And I knew Zoe was all she cared about. I knew there was only one thing I could do that would help her, and that was leave.

"I'm sorry, Jo," I said again, but she didn't move. Her back was still towards me. "I'm so sorry. I really hope everything turns out okay, but I can see you're better off without me. I'll go."

And I turned and walked out of the ward, along brightly lit corridors and out of double doors at the very end, back into the night.

I sat in Emily and wept in loathing and self-pity. I thought over everything Jo had said. It was true, wasn't it? Except that I hadn't written the book. Hadn't written a word of it. I know I'd meant to, but I couldn't when it came to it, even though I'd turned passages of it around in my head and even imagined writing them. An imaginary book isn't really a book, is it? Surely you have to actually write the words, or type them, get them on paper, before the book exists? Until then it's no more real than a daydream – a wish on the wind. But what was the real reason I hadn't typed even a single chapter? Was it my failing as an author or was it because Jo, Zoe, Baz and poor Asher had all become my closest, closest friends? They weren't just imaginary characters, paper figures placed on the map of a seaside town, moved like puppets dangling on an unreal thread, a spider's web, spun at an author's whim. They were real and what happened was real. Was that it? Or was it just because, like so many others before me, the dream of writing a book was just that – a dream? But, whatever the reason, I'd lied to them and I'd been found out. And I was in the wrong.

I found no peace or forgiveness sitting in my car in the dark, but after a while the salty tears at least stopped running down my face. I wiped my eyes and wondered what I should do. I thought of Rosmorta, on my back seat, wrapped in my sleeping bag.

"Where do you want to go?" I asked her.

I sensed no reply unless it was a vague desire for home, but where was that? I could go back to Mill Lane, but that didn't feel welcoming anymore. If I went there I'd probably just lock myself in my little attic room and not want to come out to face anybody. I could pop in briefly, pack my things before Jo returned, then drive to my parents. But their place didn't seem much like home either and I could imagine what my mother would say if I arrived unexpectedly in the middle of the night. Even popping briefly into Mill Lane I might bump into Baz. And, if I did see him, I'd ask him to tell me what he'd said to the others about my writing – about me. Ask why he hadn't told me that part of it. There'd be a row, which I didn't want to face.

In any case I couldn't leave until I found Charlie. I had to know she was alright. I mean, as alright as she could be considering her home had come crashing down around her ears. I turned the key, started Emily's engine and drove back up the cliff.

The rain had stopped and the wind had dropped. I saw the glow of a fire as I walked up from the road's end to the cottage. Flames were flickering in the outdoor pit, which we'd all sat around earlier in the summer, drinking beer and smoking and listening to music. There was only one person beside it now. I could see Charlie's outline huddled in a waterproof coat, staring at something in her hands She looked up as I approached.

"Alice, you're okay then. No one knew where you'd gone. You can see we had a disaster. Zoe's in hospital..."

I interrupted her. "I've come from there. She's unconscious. Jo's with her. Baz is at Mill Lane, he told me about the branch...

I'm so sorry about what happened. I'm sorry I wasn't there to help. Are you okay?"

"Physically, yes, okay. I'm not hurt except scratches. There's no need for you to apologise for not being there. I guess you went somewhere to shelter from the storm. At least you're safe. Do you want to sit down, share the fire? I lit it to sit beside and think."

I saw the thing Charlie was holding was a teacup, one with a sailing ship. She saw me looking at it.

"It isn't cracked. Not at all. There'll be other things to salvage, but not until it's light," she said.

"I always loved that tea set," I said.

Charlie sighed. "Yes, me too. It reminded me of my grandma, but it was more than that. It always made me think of travel. Of setting sail across the seas to somewhere I'd never been before. When I was young, I'd make up stories in my head about where I might go, what I'd do, adventures I'd have. Perhaps I'll do those things for real now, now my ties are gone."

"All you need is a tall ship and a star to steer her by..." I paraphrased.

Charlie smiled. "I didn't necessarily mean by boat, or abroad, I meant anywhere really. I could just pack my rucksack, get on my bike and ride. Just carry on going until I found somewhere I wanted to stop. Somewhere I'd never been before. Make a new life there, perhaps, or just stay for a while. Maybe that's what I will do. I always knew I wouldn't be here forever. I knew the cottage was on borrowed time, not a permanent home. I just never thought it would end like this, so soon."

"Perhaps we could get it fixed," I suggested.

"No." Charlie, shook her head. "I don't have the money. It isn't like I could have got insurance for a cottage on the cliff edge, even if I could've afforded it. Maybe I could do the work myself, patch up the roof, but it wouldn't be forever. Another few years maybe, then this whole area will have fallen into the sea. Best I'm not in it when that happens. Places don't matter, it's people who are important and the memories we take with us."

"I'm going to be leaving, too," I said. "Jo's angry with me. I can't stay."

"She'll stop being angry. She's just upset. She's the most sensible, reasonable person I know. If Zoe recovers..." Charlie paused, then went on tentatively. "Alice, what have you heard about what happened? I don't mean the branch, I mean in the séance and before it?"

"Baz told me Zoe was acting strangely," I said. Then I added, because I needed to know what really happened, "Jo said Baz talked about my writing. What did he say?"

"Hmm. Yes. Baz said something like: 'I bet this'll end up in Alice's book.' Zoe asked what he meant and he said the pair of you used to chat about your writing, when you were up at Beach View, and he was sure you'd write about us. I didn't say anything, but I agreed. I mean, we talked about that ourselves, didn't we? Personally, I think you should. Record the memories. It's the only way anyone can really live forever and not be forgotten. But Zoe hit the roof... I guess that's a poor choice of words, considering what happened. She accused you of lying over what your book was about and said maybe you shouldn't be in at the séance after all. Look, I'm sorry Alice, but I slightly agreed with her – not about the book, but because there shouldn't be disharmony in the room. I made mistakes that evening, not you, but I want to put it right."

"How do you mean?" I asked.

"I want to lay Suzie Sweet's ghost to rest for once and for all."

"How do we do that?"

"Now it's my time for confession," said Charlie. "I don't exactly know. I haven't really known what I was doing with any of this stuff. You all looked up to me, expected me to know the answers, expected me to know how to contact the dead, make dreams come true... My gran – she was a spiritualist. She took me along to séances and so on, talked to me about it. So, I knew a bit from what I heard and seen. I read a few books about magic and so on too. Plants, herbs, trees, how to make things – that's an area I do know a lot about. Magic and séances and all that stuff, not so much. But I wanted to help, and I wanted to impress, and after we found the bones it all seemed so real. After that séance, I felt I'd tapped into something, like I could do anything. I was wrong and now I've messed up. Well and truly... And what's more, I can't even find Rosmorta."

"Ah, I can help with that," I admitted. "I put her in my car, for safety, when I saw the damage at the cottage, but couldn't find anyone else there."

"That's good. I'm glad you did that. You were sensible. You should keep her, keep her safe."

"Look, there's something else I need to say, to tell you, to tell someone..." I told Charlie about what happened to me after I was sent out into the garden...was it only earlier that evening? It seemed longer. But repeating it out loud made me realise how much might have just been my imagination. Had I really sensed anything supernatural sniffing around outside the cottage? Had I really seen guiding lights in the wood? At least finding Mr Sweet had been real, and calling the ambulance. And the letter... I'd forgotten about that until now. I got it out of my pocket and showed the envelope to Charlie.

"I have to go back to Baz, don't I?" I said.

"Yes. He should open it, and he also needs to be here."

So, again, I drove to Mill Lane. I brought Baz back without any arguments and by firelight he read out the letter. I could see the look of astonishment on his face. He handed it round for Charlie and me to read too.

Baz,

I'm writing this to apologise. The guilt was mine, not yours. I was ashamed to tell you straight.

I loved Suzie, I really did, I know that now. I still see her, whatever I do to drown the memories. She's still there, wherever I look, whatever I do. I know there's nothing else for it.

I've dealt with practical matters. The paperwork. I've got no relatives, nothing else to live for.

You take care lad, you're one of the best.

Duncan Sweet

I assured Baz that Mr Sweet was still alive when the ambulance came. I told him he'd been taken to the hospital too.

"Does it change anything? I mean, anything we should do tonight, or about Suzie's ghost?" I asked.

"I'd say that's up to Baz," said Charlie.

Baz looked thoughtful, then said slowly, "I guess it depends what we're going to do."

Charlie explained that she had an idea. We still had Suzie's make-up bag. We were going to take it to the caravan site, to the charred ground where her mobile home had been. There, we would bury it and say some words as a requiem. Tell her our truth and hopefully help her rest in peace.

In the grey light of pre-dawn we stood around the small hole we'd dug in the blackened ground where that little caravan with its picket fence and gaily coloured curtains had once been. There was no one else around, and all was silent except the few words we each said in turn.

"I was your neighbour," said Charlie. "I'm sorry I never took the time to get to know you better. I place this in the ground and hope you may find solace."

She put the little bag and all its contents into the dark pit.

"I'm sorry I wished you ill," I said. "What I wished for you was wrong, and it doesn't matter if you were wrong about me, you deserved to live and you deserved a better life. We all did. I'm sorry. May you get justice and, if there is life after death, may it be all you desire."

"I loved you, Suzie," said Baz. "I'm sorry I never told you. I won't forget you. May you rest in peace."

I saw he was crying.

We covered the relics of Suzie Sweet with ash and soil, and as far as possible made it look like no one had been there. The sun was just starting to rise as we finished, looking much the same as that other dawn, when we raised Rosmorta from her cliff-side grave. Dawn is a time for new beginnings, but new beginnings also mean something older has ended. Later we learnt that at about the same time, possibly at exactly the same moment, two things happened. Zoe woke up and Mr Duncan Sweet died.

Chapter 23

Never Can Say Goodbye

A day later a letter arrived addressed to me. I'd got the job. I had to read it over twice before I believed it. After all this time, I was sure the newspaper role had been given to someone else. Actually, I later learnt that was the case. I'd been the second choice, the runner-up, kept on hold in case the first choice didn't work out. Apparently the initial lucky applicant suddenly got an even better offer a couple of weeks after starting and was off to train at one of the nationals. Of course, none of that was in my letter, which just offered me the post and asked me how soon I could start. I accepted, in a phone call to the editor from the harbour call box. I said I could start on Monday, but I needed the rest of the week to sort things out before moving back home. Yeah, home, whatever that really meant, but I did feel I had a lot still to sort out. Nevertheless, I had a job that might just be perfect after all and I was starting the next week. So little time.

Charlie didn't change her decision to move out of her cottage, but my news made her decide to delay moving on entirely. Instead, she was going to take over my attic room in Mill Lane, at least for a while. Until then she was sleeping in a tent and spending the days carefully going through her stuff, boxing up what was being moved, selling or giving away what she no longer wanted but wasn't broken, throwing out all the things that were beyond repair. The arty tourist shop that she had a regular deal with took many of the wooden trinkets that had once hung from the ceiling. The manageress even found a buyer for the driftwood table and chairs. I helped as much as I could with the clearing and packing, and transporting things I could fit in Emily.

Zoe got out of hospital after a couple of days although she was told she still had to take it easy. Jo was determined to stay by her side until she fully recovered. Charlie had been right too – Jo did forgive me and so did Zoe. We decided to have another party, a final celebration for saying goodbye, on the clifftop by Charlie's cottage before she left it for nature to take over, and before I left for my new life.

We sat around the firepit, eating food roasted in the embers, drinking beer and smoking the last of Charlie's weed. It was almost like the old times before we found the bones.

"Thank you for letting me stay with you all this summer, for helping me, for being my friends," I said.

"Are you really sure you want to go?" asked Baz. "You could stay on here, you know. It's not that much of an offer, but you could have your old job back at Beach View if you wanted it. Or a better role, help me run the place. I'm going to need help there and I'd rather work with a friend, if you were interested."

It had been confirmed that Mr Sweet had made a will just a week before he died and left the caravan site to Baz. As he'd said in the note, he had no other living relatives. Baz had been shocked and surprised. He was still trying to decide what exactly he was going to make of it all, but I think we all knew he'd make it work.

"Thanks," I said. "Part of me really wants to stay here, but I'm not going to. The newspaper's an opportunity to learn how to make a living from writing. It's what I've always wanted, what I've wished for all along. It might not be a novel, but it'll be a career. At least, I hope so. I'm glad they took so long offering me the post though. It's given me this summer, for all that's happened."

Baz nodded. "Yeah, I kinda thought you'd say that, but I wanted to offer. Look, let's not think too much about the future. Does anyone mind if I put a tape in the boom box? Not Asher's, something different to dance to?"

We all agreed that would be good and Jo smiled, the first time I'd seen her smile for so long. And we listened to music and got up and danced around the fire. We were just friends having a good time and it was perfect. Tapes end eventually though. A thought about putting them in the right cases must have crossed everyone's minds, but no one said anything even though we all seemed just a bit more thoughtful when we did it.

The words of an A-ha song on one of those tapes had taken my thoughts to that recent night in the garden when I was alone, and that dark shape I'd seen – or thought I'd seen – sniffing around the door. Perhaps my mind lingered on that for too long, or maybe it was what we'd drunk or smoked, or maybe I was picking up on something really there, because I suddenly felt a cold tingle on my skin and knew with certainty that again there was something out there. Something was watching. Something was cold and hungry and sniffing for an opportunity to get closer, out of the darkness and into our light, our company, our warm circle around the fire. And I also remembered a dream of being such a watcher, eager to join the party, but left in the shadows. I stared out into the dark wood and thought I could see something, a shape, darker than the trees and just perhaps the glimpse of yellow eyes.

"Charlie, what's that?" I tugged on her sleeve and pointed. She peered out into the trees. One by one the others stopped what they were doing and looked where we were staring.

The conversation stopped and we were silent. The noise of the wind and the rustling of autumn leaves took over. We stayed still. I don't know how long for. After a while, the shape, the dark shape, became more visible to all of us. It was low, on four legs, with shaggy black fur and big, big eyes. And it came out of the trees towards us.

"It's a dog!" Charlie broke the silence and the dog bounded up to us. She handed the mutt the burnt end of a sausage, which was wolfed down eagerly, and examined the shaggy creature who was now letting her stroke her. "She hasn't got a collar."

"She looks like she's a stray," said Zoe. "See how matted her fur is. Jo – can we keep her?"

Jo smiled. "Sure, why not?"

And so, perhaps, another of my mysteries was solved and the residents of Mill Lane took in another waif and stray.

It was the Sunday afternoon when I drove away, ready to start my new job on the Monday morning. Packed up in Emily were the possessions from my little room in one rucksack and a few cardboard boxes, pretty much as I'd arrived for my summer by the sea. Charlie continued to insist that I should be the guardian of Rosmorta, her skull and bones and little grave goods. She also gave me the little wooden cupboard with its lock and key: Rosmorta's shrine and a neat bookcase too. In it, I'd used my sleeping bag to pack everything safe. Zoe gave me the picture she'd sketched of that beach scene, of a bay with bands of sand and shingle and a tall white cliff with trees at the top, the one that's still on my wall as I write this, foxed and faded but still haunting. In return, I gave Zoe my typewriter so she could make neat labels for the pictures she was going to paint and sell in the future.

They all came out to wish me goodbye: Jo, Zoe, Baz, Charlie and the new dog, who they'd named Jenny. For a moment, in the corner of my eye, it seemed there was another figure there with them but just to one side. I caught just a glimpse of a baggy shirt in a bold print. It was probably my imagination as with so many things that summer. The mind can easily play tricks and memory is fickle too.

I kept in touch with my friends at Mill Lane for a while, mostly by letters and cards as we did back in the days before social media or even email. Charlie's cottage was a victim of the

Great Storm just a few weeks after the one that broke the fateful branch. A huge chunk of cliff fell away, taking the remains of her home with it, and I was grateful to the earlier storm and the branch for meaning that Charlie wasn't in the cottage when it fell, but was tucked up safe in my old attic room.

Epilogue

Always on My Mind

Over the years I've thought a lot about whether any of the magic of that summer really affected what would have happened anyway. I've often pondered whether we can tempt fate or change fate. If fate's a thing, then I think we can change it if we try, but I'm still not sure that I really believe in fate at all. Mostly it's the choices and actions made by people doing real things in the real world that make a difference. It isn't so much whether we wish someone ill, as whether we do anything to harm them. Let's face it, we've probably all wished people were dead once or twice in our lives and mostly those people live to ripe old ages and continue to do things other people wish they hadn't. Working on a newspaper, that kind of thing's mostly what you get to write about. Nevertheless, I do still believe that if you will something hard enough, it might just make a bit of difference, and I've learnt my lesson to be careful what I asked for.

So why have I written this book now, after all these years? Why didn't I just let sleeping dogs lie? Well, recently I've been having this dream that brought it all back. In my dream I return to that rundown seaside town, only it isn't like that anymore. The rows of Victorian houses have mostly been done up and gentrified again. Once more it's fashionable for people from the city go there for weekends away to enjoy walks along the promenade and oysters and local beers in quaint harbour-side pubs. But in my dream, I drive past the harbour and the tourists and take the road up the cliff to its very end. The end is nearer now, but I park my car, and from the back I unwrap Rosmorta – her skull and bones and little grave goods. With them in my arms, I walk to the edge of the cliff. I stand looking over the sea, wondering why I've come there. Then I know, and I have this urge to hurl the skull and the bones and everything else to the wind, to tumble down the cliff to smash on the rocks, where they would have smashed so many years ago, and be carried out to sea on a swelling current.

But I don't do it straight away. I stand and watch. I look down. Instead of rocks lashed by breakers I see a beach below with bands of sand and shingle, and the tide is out. I see a child playing at the edge of the water. She's built a sandcastle and is defending it against the incoming waves. I watch for a long time, rapt by the child's determination in the face of the inundation which is slowly but inexorably washing away at its foundations. And I realise that I do have a choice, and I choose not to spoil that child's moment with my actions. I turn and walk away.

We all have dreams. I mean things we wish for and want as well as the kind we have when we're asleep. We should all get a chance for our wishes and dreams to come true. Sometimes we have to wait a long time for that to happen and sometimes we have to work hard towards achieving our goals. Even if a dream has lain dormant, buried for years, it's never too late to resurrect it and make it real, if that's what we truly want. And so I'm writing this book, because I believe that people are important and recording our memories of them is the only way they can truly survive the efforts of the sands of time to erode them.

Bestsellers from Moon Books

Keeping Her Keys
An Introduction to Hekate's Modern Witchcraft
Cyndi Brannen
Blending Hekate, witchcraft and personal development together to create a powerful new magickal perspective.
Paperback: 978-1-78904-075-3 ebook 978-1-78904-076-0

Journey to the Dark Goddess
How to Return to Your Soul
Jane Meredith
Discover the powerful secrets of the Dark Goddess and transform your depression, grief and pain into healing and integration.
Paperback: 978-1-84694-677-6 ebook: 978-1-78099-223-5

Shamanic Reiki
Expanded Ways of Working with Universal Life Force Energy
Llyn Roberts, Robert Levy
Shamanism and Reiki are each powerful ways of healing; together, their power multiplies. Shamanic Reiki introduces techniques to help healers and Reiki practitioners tap ancient healing wisdom.
Paperback: 978-1-84694-037-8 ebook: 978-1-84694-650-9

Southern Cunning
Folkloric Witchcraft in the American South
Aaron Oberon
Modern witchcraft with a Southern flair, this book is a journey through the folklore of the American South and a look at the power these stories hold for modern witches.
Paperback: 978-1-78904-196-5 ebook: 978-1-78904-197-2

Readers of ebooks can buy or view any of these bestsellers by clicking on the live link in the title. Most titles are published in paperback and as an ebook. Paperbacks are available in traditional bookshops. Both print and ebook formats are available online.

Find more titles and sign up to our readers' newsletter
http://www.johnhuntpublishing.com/paganism

For video content, author interviews and more, please subscribe to our YouTube channel.

MoonBooksPublishing

Follow us on social media for book news, promotions and more:

Facebook: Moon Books Publishing

Instagram: @moonbooksjhp

Twitter: @MoonBooksJHP

Tik Tok: @moonbooksjhp